Lucy Monroe

WEDDING VOW
OF REVENGE

Bedded by...

Forced to bed...then to wed?

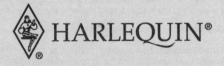

HARLEQUIN®

TORONTO • NEW YORK • LONDON
AMSTERDAM • PARIS • SYDNEY • HAMBURG
STOCKHOLM • ATHENS • TOKYO • MILAN • MADRID
PRAGUE • WARSAW • BUDAPEST • AUCKLAND

ISBN 0-373-12526-7

WEDDING VOW OF REVENGE

First North American Publication 2006.

Copyright © 2005 by Lucy Monroe.

www.eHarlequin.com

Printed in U.S.A.

All about the author...
Lucy Monroe

Award-winning and bestselling author **LUCY MONROE** sold her first book in September 2002 to the Harlequin Presents line. That book represented a dream that had been burning in her heart for years: the dream to share her stories with readers who love romance as much as she does. Since then she has sold more than thirty books to three publishers and hit national bestseller lists in the U.S. and England. But what has touched her most deeply since selling that first book are the reader letters she receives. Her most important goal with every book is to touch a reader's heart and when she hears she's done that it makes every night spent writing into the wee hours of morning worth it.

She started reading Harlequin Presents books very young and discovered a heroic type of man between the covers of those books—an honorable man, capable of faithfulness and sacrifice for the people he loves. Now married to what she terms her "alpha male at the end of a book," Lucy believes there is a lot more reality to the fantasy stories she writes than most people give credit for. She believes in happy endings that are really marvelous beginnings and that's why she writes them. She hopes her books help readers to believe a little, too...just like romance did for her so many years ago.

She really does love to hear from readers and esponds to every e-mail. You can reach her by e-mailing lucymonroe@lucymonroe.com.

For my Grandmother Lucille and my Great Aunts...
you are women who have inspired me my whole life
with your wit, your work ethic, your intelligence,
your generosity and your zest for living. I want to
thank you for that from the very depths of my heart.
I love you all. Blessings, Lucy

CHAPTER ONE

ANGELO GORDON'S blue eyes narrowed with interest.

"You're sure of this information, *amico mio*?" he demanded, his American accent spiced with Sicilian overtones that denoted his reaction to the news more strongly than words could have.

Hawk nodded. "Positive. Baron Randall has been keeping tabs on Tara Peters since their affair ended two years ago."

"How did you find out?"

"The owner of the security agency Randall has on retainer talks more than he should after a couple of whiskey sours." Hawk didn't make those kinds of mistakes, but didn't mind taking advantage when someone else did.

"That's convenient."

"I thought so."

"Okay. Give me the scoop and don't leave anything out."

Hawk tossed the file on Angelo's desk and waited for the tall Sicilian-American to open it.

He pointed to the news story on top that showed his client's enemy with his arm around a woman more than a decade his junior. "Randall and Miss Peters met four years ago at a fashion show in New York. He was there with another model, but left with Miss Peters. By all accounts, he swept the young Miss Peters off her feet and into his bed. She gave up modeling and started taking college courses. They were together for eighteen months and broke up when he became engaged to his current wife. Rumor suggests he asked Miss Peters to remain his mistress."

"She refused."

"Yes."

"She was stronger than my mother." Grudging respect laced Angelo's voice. "Why is he having her watched?"

"According to my informant, Randall still wants her. He's given instructions to scotch any possible romantic entanglements. So far, my colleague hasn't had to make the effort."

Angelo surged to his feet and turned to look out the window behind his desk. His brooding six-foot-two-inch frame blocked the light and Hawk's view of upper Manhattan. "What the hell does he expect to accomplish? That's what I want to know."

"Obviously reentrance into her life."

Angelo turned back, his patrician features creased with a frown of disbelief. "That doesn't make any sense. She said no and apparently meant it."

"Right. It makes one wonder how long Baron Randall expected his marriage to last in the first place.

When he married, his wife's father had been recently diagnosed with an inoperable heart condition."

"But good living and exercise have given him a clean bill of health, or at least a new lease on life."

Hawk smiled cynically. "Much to Randall's dismay no doubt. The marriage has never been a happy one."

For which Angelo could take some credit.

Tara wasn't the only woman Randall had propositioned for the role of his mistress. Others had accepted and thanks to some judicious behind the scenes handling on both Hawk and Angelo's part, the young Mrs. Randall knew it.

"According to my sources, she will be filing for divorce within the month."

Angelo inclined his head in acknowledgment of information that would not have come as a surprise. "You think he wants to take up where he left off when he's free?"

"I can see no other explanation for his behavior. Miss Peters is the only long-term relationship Baron Randall has had in more than a decade that did not profit him business wise. He cheated on her only when he was away from her. For an amoral womanizer like him, that is bloody significant."

Hawk had never before seen Angelo Gordon wearing that particular expression. *"You think he loves her?"*

"Love?" Hawk flicked his hand in a dismissive gesture. "Not bloody likely, but I do think he's obsessed by her. From what information I can gather, she is unique, if only in her ability to walk away from him. My instincts tell me it's more than that, though. She was very

career minded as a model. He was her first serious boy-friend."

"You think she was a virgin when they met? *How old is she?*"

"Twenty-four and yes, I think Randall's the only lover she's ever had."

"That does make her unique, especially in Randall's jaded world."

"There's more."

"What?"

"You aren't going to believe this." Hawk had had a hard time believing it himself. "It is simply too damn perfect."

"And *it* is?"

"She graduated with her degree in business six months ago and has been in Primo Tech's management training program for the past four of those months."

Angelo had bought the hi-tech company in Portland, Oregon, three years ago. Just like all the other companies he bought and resuscitated, it was becoming a lead player in its industry. However, the success of his company was no doubt not nearly as interesting to him in that moment as the fact Tara Peters was employed there.

"It's fate."

Hawk's laugh was every bit as skeptical as Angelo's. "That is one way of looking at it."

Angelo sat at his desk after Hawk left, perusing the file on Tara Peters. Hawk had included still shots from several of her fashion shows. They showed a woman of ethereal beauty, shrouded by innocence, but wearing clothing that would tempt a saint to sin. On her tall, model slim body, that nevertheless had curves in all the right places, they were more than a temptation…they were downright provocation.

Her dark brown eyes in the perfectly proportioned oval face, surrounded by a cascade of silky chestnut hair intrigued him…even knowing she had once been Baron Randall's.

He flipped through the photos until he came to those included with the tabloid articles that had sensationalized her breakup with Randall. The difference between the two sets of pictures wrenched at something inside Angelo he thought long dead. Those same chocolate-dark eyes now reflected the pain of betrayal and lost innocence.

Just like his mother's had.

He needed to assimilate this piece of information and decide how best to act on it. He didn't have much time, either. If for no other reason than that Baron Randall would go looking for Tara Peters the minute his wife filed the divorce petition.

That gave Angelo a month, maybe less to act on his newfound knowledge of Randall's unexpected weakness.

The man who had stolen his company and destroyed his mother deserved to be ruined on every level and Angelo was going to make damn sure that happened.

Tara Peters laughed at the other junior execs around her, at least the female ones. They were primping for the arrival of Angelo Gordon like he was a rock star or something.

"Aren't you even going to put on lipstick?" Danette Michaels demanded with her usual forthrightness after glossing her own lips and putting her compact mirror away in her desk drawer. "He's supposed to do a tour of this floor sometime today."

"No lipstick." Tara had spent years wearing just the right makeup, dressing with flair, and flaunting the assets that had made her a top model at the age of twenty.

They had also brought her to the notice of Baron Randall and for that alone, she would spend the rest of her life devoid of makeup and dressing in conservative business attire.

Never again.

She straightened the papers on her desk. "My only interest in impressing Mr. Gordon is with my work and I don't need lipstick to do it."

Danette rolled her eyes. "You are such an all work and no play kind of girl. Did you ever hear that makes you boring and can give you ulcers before you're thirty?"

Coming from a woman who had her first serious boyfriend at the age of twenty-one, that was pretty funny.

"My twenty-four-year-old stomach is just fine, thank you and better boring than stomped on I always say."

"Not every man in the world is like that jerk, Baron Randall."

Like most people, Danette had read the tabloid accounts of Tara getting dumped by Baron so he could marry his oil heiress. However, unlike most people, the younger woman had not let the stories color her view of Tara. She thought Baron was a world class pig and that her friend was better off without him.

Tara agreed. Now.

But two years ago, she'd felt like she would die from the pain and humiliation of the all too public breakup.

"Of course they aren't," she said, trying to stave off another lecture about getting back on the horse so she wouldn't forget how to ride. Between Danette and her mother, she'd heard it about a thousand times too many. "But right now I'm not interested in finding out. I don't have time for a man in my life and honestly, I don't see how you can, either."

Danette shrugged, her amber cat eyes twinkling.

"Some of us are better at multitasking than others," she said with a grin. "Anyway, even if your career is all you care about, you should want to make a good impression on Angelo Gordon. He owns this company and several like it."

"I do want to impress him…with my business acumen."

"He's already impressed, Tara."

Tara spun in her chair to face her manager, surprised Mr. Curtiss was here instead of in the schmoozing session with the upper managers and the company owner.

"Mr. Gordon wants to speak to you privately."

Tension stiffened her spine as the words reminded her of a similar conversation she'd had with her modeling agent. The woman had told her that Baron Randall wanted to meet her. Tara, naïve idiot that she had been four years ago, had been both flattered and impressed.

"Why alone?"

If her manager thought that an odd question, he

didn't let it show. "He's impressed with your report on workplace effectiveness. He wants to discuss it with you."

Relaxing, she smiled. Business. It was just about business, nothing like that other time when the introduction had been a prelude to seduction.

"That's great, Tara," Danette said, "I heard the guy is a genius. If he appreciates your brains already, I guess it's true."

"Does he want to see me right now?" she asked, feeling a little light-headed.

Sure, she'd daydreamed about the owner of the company being so impressed with her recommendations he wanted to talk to her. What junior executive didn't? But that kind of stuff didn't happen in the real world.

Her manager looked at his watch and frowned. "Five minutes ago, actually. I got waylaid by a phone call on my way to tell you."

Tara Peters walked into Angelo's temporary office with her back straight and a credible expression of confidence. The only giveaway to her nervousness at being summoned by the owner of the company was the tight clenching of her fingers into small fists at her sides.

Her bone structure was delicate for a woman of her height, which no doubt explained her success as a catwalk model.

Yet, she looked very different from the still shots of her fashion shows that Hawk had included in the *Tara Peters* file. Nor did she resemble the pictures that had accompanied the tabloid articles after her breakup with Randall.

All the photos had shown a stunning woman who made the most of her beauty, but no one would accuse this Tara Peters of trading on her beauty to succeed in her job.

She had confined the glorious length of her signature chestnut hair in a tight French braid that fell down her back. She wore no makeup and the small ovals of her nails were unpolished, but buffed. The navy-blue slacks and blazer she wore disguised her figure very well.

He hadn't been sure what to expect, but her current no-nonsense, almost androgynous attire fit Hawk's report on her behavior since Baron Randall married another woman.

Tara didn't date and appeared uninterested in attracting men. Was she still hung up on the monster? The thought did not sit well with Angelo and his usually impassive face creased in a frown before he realized it.

"Mr. Gordon?" The voice was questioning, but not hesitant and he liked that.

He admired strength because weakness…of any kind…cost far too much.

He looked up and met her faintly quizzical brown eyes. "Miss Peters. Please take a seat."

She moved across the room and slid gracefully into a chair opposite his desk. His opinion changed on the suit. The jacket dipped in at her waist. Her movement had revealed curves that were neither pronounced nor were they so slight her blouse could disguise them completely. The way the clothes tried to hide, but could not help hinting at her femininity made him want to strip them off and see the beautiful body beneath.

It did not help that pictures from her file of her clad in bikinis and other almost-there outfits flashed in his mind's eye.

Desire vibrated through him with shocking swiftness and urgency, making him glad for the concealment of his desk. He hadn't responded with this level of physical intensity to the mere sight of a woman since puberty.

He forced his mind through the mental exercises he had learned in the Aikido training he had started as a young boy. He continued to train, using it as a way to keep his body fit and mind focused. Normally it worked without him even having to think about.

This time, he had to wait for the stunning response of his body to subside breath by breath before he could begin to concentrate on his agenda. "I've been reading your report on workplace effectiveness. You've drawn several interesting conclusions and made an equal number of suggestions that are worthy of note."

Her eyes lit with pleasure and she smiled, her feminine fragrance teasing his nostrils as she leaned forward. "There's a wealth of data to be analyzed and interpreted from recent studies on the subject, much of which has been ignored by current management theory."

He nodded. Whatever else Miss Peters was, she had shown herself to be a natural in her chosen field. "I particularly found your suggestions regarding vacation time of interest."

"Several studies have shown that employees who put in less overtime, take their vacation yearly and don't consistently work through their lunch hours are actually more productive than their counterparts who work the longer hours and never take any time off." She smiled. "Healthier, too. They have fewer heart attacks and are less likely to develop ulcers."

"You've definitely done your homework."

She blushed at the compliment and he filed the reaction away for future reference. From the way she presented herself, he had to assume her beauty was of much less significance to her than doing well at her job.

Interesting.

And unusual.

"Many of your suggestions fly in the face of corporate policies the world over."

She leaned further forward in her chair, her oval face animated and flushed in a way he'd like to see somewhere besides the boardroom. "Those management styles are as outdated as the all-male executive staff. They don't work in today's dynamic workforce, particularly the organic environment found in the hi-tech industry."

"Why did you go for a job in hi-tech? Your résumé shows a strong liberal arts background for your business degree."

She looked disconcerted by his question and settled back in her chair, biting her lip uncertainly. "The job description did not include a requirement in technological education."

"I'm aware of that, but you did not answer my question."

She smiled slightly. "Sorry. You're right." Her smile grew and her demeanor relaxed. "I like the stimulating atmosphere. Things are always changing, not just the products, but the face of the workforce as well. The job is challenging. But most importantly, I wanted to work someplace I could make a difference."

"And you thought Primo Tech would be it?"

"Yes."

He lifted the report that would have caught his attention even if it hadn't been the ideal conduit for their first meeting. "I would say you are well on your way to doing so."

"I'm glad you think so." She beamed and he found himself smiling in return, something he rarely did.

His phone buzzed at exactly the moment he had instructed his secretary to ring through.

He lifted the receiver. "Gordon here."

"Mr. Gordon, I'm ringing as instructed."

"Thank you. And my other arrangements?"

"The reservations are made. Dinner at seven-thirty in the restaurant of your hotel."

"Hold on just a moment." He pressed the hold button and schooled his face into an apologetic expression, another one he used infrequently. "I'm sorry, I have to take this call."

Tara stood hurriedly. "Of course."

She was halfway to the door when he said, "Miss Peters."

She turned. "Yes?"

"I would like to discuss the report further. Can you meet me this evening for a business dinner at my hotel?"

Despite the fact he had specifically referred to it as business, her eyes filled with wariness. "Dinner?"

"Yes. Is that a problem?" he asked, inflecting his voice with just the right amount of superiority and disapproval to remind her who he was.

She took a deep breath and squared her shoulders, her lips flattened in a determined line. "No. I'll be there. What hotel and what time?"

He told her and then watched her walk out of his office, his attention on the way her slacks outlined her heart-shaped behind. This aspect of his plan for revenge was shaping up to be more pleasure than work.

Seducing Tara Peters would be no hardship at all.

Tara got ready for dinner, her nerves more on edge than they had been in two long years. Why? Because the minute another magnetic, sexy tycoon came on the scene, her body had started reacting. She couldn't believe it and was thoroughly disgusted with herself.

Worse, she'd seen immediately the unexpected feelings of attraction were mutual. She might have very little practical experience with men, but she'd been on the receiving end often enough to identify when a man was attracted to her. She'd learned early in her modeling career to recognize and avoid it.

Her one failure being both spectacular and devastating.

She hadn't spent the last two years avoiding men and entanglements just to fall for another Baron Randall. No way. She was smarter than that.

Even brief contemplation of a relationship with a man like Angelo Gordon would be stupidity itself.

Right. Remember that.

Only instincts that had nothing to do with intelligence and everything to do with emotion were sending all sorts of messages to her brain. They urged her to put on a little makeup, change into a more feminine dress and brush out her long hair for goodness sake! She'd done her best to sublimate such impulses for two years.

Her mind said now was not the time for a resurrection, but her heart and body said otherwise.

Stupid, stupid, stupid, she muttered under her breath as she put the final pin in the sleek French roll on the back of her head and surveyed her appearance. She'd changed her slacks for a black skirt and her blouse and blazer for a matching jacket meant to be worn buttoned up as a top.

With her understated black heels and sheer stockings, she had a distinctly Jackie-O appearance without the feminine softening of lipstick and accent jewelry.

Perfect.

No way could her boss misinterpret her outfit as any sort of attempt to entice him on a personal level.

She didn't care if Angelo Gordon affected her in ways she'd thought deadened by Baron's betrayal. Wanting him scared her far more than it enticed her and she wasn't giving into it.

Desire was an emotion that encouraged smart women to make dumb decisions.

Hadn't she seen that enough growing up with her mom bouncing from one destructive relationship to the next? Her mom had never understood why none of the men stayed. She hadn't comprehended that the type of powerful, charismatic male she was attracted to traded on those very traits to get what he wanted—sex with a beautiful woman.

However, they'd all been incapable of giving her mom what *she* needed…love.

Tara's mom had only broken the cycle by default when miracle of miracles, a strong, sexy man also turned out to have a heart.

It was Darren Colby's influence in Tara's life that had led her to believe that kind of man wasn't always bad news. She was no longer so naïve. Darren was an anomaly in the male species, an alpha male with a heart…but she didn't figure anomalies like that came along more than maybe once a millennium.

She would stay focused on her job and not the way Angelo Gordon's dark good looks affected her libido.

Tara walked into the posh downtown hotel, projecting an unshakable confidence that was only skin deep. Inside, she was as nervous as she'd been her first day on the job. More even, because then all she'd been fighting was a fear of the unknown. Tonight, she fought her fear of being weak.

Angelo waited for her at a table in a small private alcove of the hotel restaurant. A historic landmark, the hotel's rich décor of carved wood paneling leading to cavernously high ceilings was original to its nineteenth century construction. Despite the distance to the ceilings, the rich detail of the da Vinci-like scenes painted there caught her attention.

But even the artwork's beauty could not keep her focus when she could feel Angelo's regard across the restaurant. He watched her with unreadable blue eyes as she made her way toward him between linen topped tables graced by well dressed diners. Even from this far away, he exerted an aura of masculine power that sent her heart tripping.

Just like Baron.

Only unlike Baron, she would not allow herself to be fooled into believing Angelo was more than what he appeared on the surface, a ruthless corporate shark.

He stood when she reached the table, his height startling at close quarters. At five foot nine, she was no shrimp, but the top of her head barely reached his shoulder.

She had to tilt her head back to look him in the eye. It was a very odd feeling. "Good evening, Mr. Gordon."

He waited for the maître d' to seat her before sitting down again. "Angelo, please. I prefer a more relaxed environment in my companies."

"Your approach appears to be quite effective. You've never lost a company yet."

Something swirled in his indigo gaze as he poured her a glass of wine from the bottle already sitting on the table. "Actually, I have lost one, but that was a long time ago."

Sensing he had no desire to discuss it further, she took a sip of the fruity wine and then asked, "Angelo is an Italian name?"

Other than the blue eyes, which were not entirely uncommon in Italian men—with his dark hair and tanned good looks, he had a very Mediterranean appearance.

"My mother was Sicilian."

That explained a lot, but remembering a fashion shoot she'd done outside of Palermo one summer, she said, "Most Sicilian men are a lot shorter than you."

"My father was American."

"And tall," she guessed.

He smiled, making her breath catch. This man was beautiful.

"Yes. According to my mother, that was one of the first things she noticed about him. There was more than a foot disparity in their sizes, but I can never remember them seeming like they did not fit."

"I've heard love can be a great equalizer," she said with a tinge of mockery she wished she didn't feel.

But after her childhood and one disastrous personal affair, she had little belief in the emotion so many touted as the panacea for all ills.

"So they say." His tone was no less cynical than her own.

The waiter came to take their order and she made a point of selecting her own meal. This was not a date and even if it was, she didn't go in for the old world custom of the male ordering for the female. She'd spent too many years taking care of herself.

"You wanted to discuss my report?" she asked after the waiter left.

"First, I think I should like to know a little more about you, Tara."

"I'm sure all the pertinent information is in my employee record."

"Perhaps I prefer to hear it firsthand."

"I was under the impression this was supposed to be

a business dinner." She kept her tone light, not wanting to offend her boss, but not so light he wouldn't take the comment to heart.

His midnight gaze caressed her with tactile force and it was all she could do not to shiver. "My closest friends started as business associates."

"You don't strike me as a man with a lot of close friends." She'd meant the words to come out worldly and sophisticated, but instead her voice was two octaves lower than normal and sounded flirtatious, darn it.

"You're very perceptive." He cocked his head slightly, his expression challenging her. "That does not mean you could not become one of them."

"You're very bold."

"I didn't get where I am hesitating to go after what I want."

"If you want my business expertise, you can have it. If you're looking for a personal relationship with an employee, I decline." She couldn't be more direct than that, but then this man apparently needed blunt.

He nodded, his expression showing no offence. "I can respect that." Then he smiled. "That does not mean I won't try to change your mind."

"I would prefer if you didn't."

"I would prefer you did not treat me like a pariah simply because I own the company you work for."

"Wanting to stick to business is hardly treating you like an outcast."

"And denying me the possibility of friendship?"

"You don't need my friendship."

"You are wrong." And the intensity in his expression said he was telling her the truth, but how could that be?

Unless his definition of friendship and hers were not quite the same thing. Maybe he was between *girlfriends* at the moment.

"I have no interest in becoming a business tycoon's pillow friend."

CHAPTER TWO

"DO YOU judge every man you meet by Baron Randall's standards?"

She should not be surprised he knew about her past. Half the modern world had read the tabloid stories. Or at least it seemed that way sometimes. It was a good thing she'd learned early on in her modeling career that someone asking an awkward or painful question did not equate to an obligation on her part to answer it.

"That's really none of your business, Mr. Gordon."

"Angelo."

She barely refrained from rolling her eyes. "Angelo. I work for you and to my knowledge a personal relationship with my employer is not a requirement on my job description."

His amused but piercing gaze did things to her insides she desperately wished it didn't. "You are not only forthright, but you're damn certain of yourself."

"Yes." He wasn't the only person who knew what he wanted and went for it. Rather she knew what she didn't want—a repeat of her disastrous affair with a ruthless business tycoon.

Despite the fact that Angelo made a pointed effort to restrain his conversation to her business report over dinner, Tara found herself unwillingly enthralled by the man himself. He was intense, dynamic and smart. Smarter than any person she'd ever met and yet, he didn't dismiss her opinions if they differed from his. She appreciated that more than he could know, truly enjoying the evidence that he respected her even if she wasn't quite in his league.

That was something she'd always felt was in doubt in her relationship with Baron.

She hadn't been sure how Angelo would take her not-so-gentle refusal to get personal, but he'd responded with a professionalism and maturity she couldn't help admiring. She'd known men a lot older than him that reverted to spoiled little boys when thwarted in their pursuit of a woman.

For that reason, she found herself relaxing as the evening progressed, less concerned when their conversation took temporary by-ways not related wholly to human resource management.

They'd spent an hour over dinner before she even realized it.

The waiter asked if they wanted dessert and Angelo looked at her. "Do you have a sweet tooth? I've had their raspberry crème brûlée and it is some of the best I've tasted anywhere."

"Crème brûlée is my favorite," she admitted, her mouth watering at the prospect of indulging in the treat.

With one of his rare, but devastating smiles, he ordered one for each of them.

The desserts arrived and she had to stifle an animal groan of anticipation when she saw the perfect caramelization of the glaze on top.

"You look like you've just been offered a dish of ambrosia."

"Haven't I?"

He laughed, the sound doing things to her even more insidious than the sight of the decadent treat.

She felt compelled to explain her over the top reaction. "I spent years eschewing refined sugar and processed food of any kind for the benefit of my figure and complexion."

Appreciative eyes burned over her and she felt like she was wearing a spandex mini that revealed every curve rather than the black Jackie-O suit.

"You must still refrain quite a bit." His voice caressed her with obvious masculine approval.

For the first time in years, she found herself blushing about a comment made regarding her physical appearance. She'd gotten very used to seeing her body as her tool in trade, but this man made her very aware of herself as a feminine being.

She shrugged, projecting the air of insouciance she *should* be feeling about his comment. "I didn't stop modeling all that long ago."

His eyes narrowed. "I was under the impression you came to Primo Tech straight out of college."

"I did, but the last couple of years I supported myself with my modeling."

"After your breakup with Randall."

She grimaced. "Yes."

"He paid for your schooling before that?"

She didn't know why, but she found herself wanting to answer his question, when normally she would have cut such personal conversation off at the knees.

"He wanted to maximize our time together, so I agreed not to work."

"I'm surprised he didn't want you to give up school."

"Oh, he did." But as much as she'd thought she loved the swine, she'd been unwilling to give up her independence completely, or her dreams for her future.

"You refused."

"Adamantly."

"Did you retire from modeling because he wanted you to?"

Again, the question didn't offend her so much as give her an opportunity to talk about something she'd kept locked away inside for two long years. "I'd always planned on retiring young enough to go to school and move onto a second career. So, when he said he wanted to be the only man in my life, not one in a cast of thousands, I agreed and quit a few years and a few goals before I'd planned to. I was actually flattered he felt so strongly."

She knew her voice echoed her disgust with herself over her naiveté. Even so, her insistence on taking college courses had been a bone of contention between them until their break-up.

"Do you regret that decision?"

"I find regret a wasted emotion. When I had to go

back to work to support myself again, it was harder to get the lucrative jobs, but I survived and I learned a lot in the process."

Angelo studied her, what looked like real respect warming his gaze. "Yet even after going back to work, you excelled in your studies. I have heard modeling requires a great deal of dedication."

No doubt he'd dated a few models in his time. Most rich men did, seeing beautiful women as adornments as surely as designers saw models as mannequins to display their wares.

Still, she couldn't help liking the knowledge he was impressed with her efforts at school rather than offended by them as Baron had been.

"I don't think I could have modeled full-time and gone to school as well, but I earned enough working through the summers to support myself during the school year."

"You're a very determined woman."

"I'd say that was something you probably understand well."

"You'd be right." He pointed his spoon toward her brûlée. "Taste."

Did he have any idea what the sexy timbre of his voice did to her insides? Of course not, and no way was she letting on either. Better to get over the strange, melting reaction than expose it in any way, but every word was like foreplay to her sexually deprived body.

Bad. This was very bad.

She grabbed her spoon, conversation ceasing while she obeyed his order to taste. She gave a helpless moan of pleasure as the first bite of the perfectly prepared sweet filled her senses. Her eyes closed and she savored the taste she indulged in so rarely.

She'd once had another model describe a chocolate torte as orgasmic, but until this moment she'd never had an erotic reaction to food before. The sensual slide of the vanilla custard across her tongue was just that though and goose bumps formed on her inner thighs as her womb clenched in an astonishing reaction to the delicacy.

Belatedly coming to terms with how her not-so-innocent enjoyment could be misinterpreted, she quickly opened her eyes. Straightening in her chair, she tried to wipe the pleasure from her expression and willed her unruly body to calm down.

Her spoon clattered to the table in her haste to let it go. "Um, it's very good. You were right." She forced her gaze to meet his, afraid of what she would see, but unwilling to play the coward. "I guess I got a little carried away there."

Blue eyes looked back at her with hunger, but he shook his head. "Relax. You look like you think I'm going to pounce."

"Aren't you?" She wasn't an idiot and she wasn't a tease. She knew what her reaction had to have looked like to him.

A total come-on, despite all she'd said about not wanting to get involved.

"You've made your view of a relationship between the two of us very clear, Tara." He spoke as if instructing a small child and perversely she wanted to tell him she was anything but. "I'm not going to read an invitation in a former model's obvious love of feeding her starved sweet tooth."

"Thank you." And she should feel grateful. Extremely grateful.

Not disappointed.

"No problem. Now, enjoy your dessert."

He'd let her off the hook with his assurance, so why did she feel even further enmeshed in his web than before?

"So, how was dinner?" Danette asked in a low undertone as she and Tara worked on slides for a presentation their manager was supposed to give to Angelo and the top management string the following morning.

Tara looked around, thankful no one was nearby enough to overhear her friend's question. The dinner last night had been strictly business, but that wasn't necessarily how others would interpret it.

After her affair with Baron, she'd been the butt of enough gossip to last her a lifetime. "Shh. I don't want to talk about it right now."

Danette's hazel eyes widened, darkening to green with a knowing gleam. "So it wasn't just business."

"No," Tara snapped, then realized her answer had come out wrong. "I mean yes…I mean it *was* business and *only* business." If she didn't count the orgasmic dessert. "Okay?"

"I don't know. Angelo Gordon is a real hottie and you seem pretty frazzled for a woman who had a *strictly business* date last night."

"It wasn't *a date* at all."

"Are you saying he didn't make a move on you?"

How did she answer that? Had their conversation at the beginning of dinner been a move? She thought maybe it had, but then he'd backed off pretty easily.

She took too long to answer and Danette's expression turned gleefully calculating. "So, he is attracted to you."

That was something she couldn't deny without lying. "Could we drop this discussion? We've got work to do."

"Sure, but, hon, just answer one question…if last night was all business and no play, why are you blushing to the roots of your gorgeous hair?"

Tara still hadn't come up with an adequate reply to her friend's teasing comment by the time the other woman left work to get ready for her very real date with a budding journalist.

It had bugged her all day. For something like the hundredth time since waking that morning, she shoved thoughts of Angelo to the back of her mind. She forced herself to concentrate on the papers in front of her.

With no distractions around her and fierce effort, it worked. She was so engrossed that security came to tell her all external entrances but the main one had been secured for the evening before she realized what time it was. She looked at her watch and was shocked to see it was well after seven.

She should have left over two hours ago.

Muscles cramped from long hours of sitting in the same position protested and she stood to stretch. Her tummy growled, but her eyes were drawn back to the almost completed report on her desk. Just another hour or so and she would be done.

"Why are you still here?"

She jumped at the sound of Angelo's voice, her entire body flushing with warmth and she hadn't even turned to look at him.

When she did, she felt like she'd been hit by a truck. Why did the man have to be so darn sexy? Most of his management team was at least a decade older, balding and showing the effects of middle age in their belt size, but not Angelo. He was tall and lean with muscles to die for and if he was much over thirty, she'd eat the report she'd been editing.

"I was working on a project and got lost to the time."

"What about this workplace effectiveness model you've been trying to sell to management? Doesn't that include going home on time?"

She shrugged guiltily. "Theory doesn't always work in reality."

He smiled, white teeth flashing in his gorgeous face. "No, it doesn't, but if you're going to convince my management team of your theories, you're going to have to live and work by them."

"You're right, of course." She sighed, wishing life was as easy as putting ideas down on paper. "I guess you got caught up in something, too?"

His expression cooled for no reason she could discern. "I was putting together the plans for a new acquisition."

"You're buying another company?"

Satisfaction flashed in his eyes, but they remained strangely chilled. "Yes."

"Um…congratulations."

"Thank you." He ran his fingers through the short, dark curls on his head, leaving them mussed and looking way too enticing for her own good. "Have you had dinner?"

"No. I'll stop and get something on the way home." She turned and grabbed her suit jacket off the hook on the cubicle wall behind her desk.

As she did so, she realized the sheer white camisole that looked perfectly acceptable under the jacket was much too thin for a business environment without it. It had gotten warm and she hadn't even been aware of taking the jacket off, but now she wished she hadn't gotten quite so engrossed in her work.

Looking down, she could see the shadow of nipples that had hardened upon her boss's arrival and was darn sure he could, too.

"Have dinner with me." His voice betrayed nothing, but he made no pretense of ignoring the display. Dark indigo eyes flicked from her breasts to her face. "Well?"

Sensation zinged through her, making her tight peaks sting and she shoved her arms into the sleeves of her suit jacket.

Panicked at how tempting the invitation was and the desperate reaction of her body, she blurted the first excuse that came to her mind. "I'm really not all that hungry."

Her stomach gave immediate lie to her words with an audible growl and she had to bite back a groan of embarrassment.

"Are you sure about that?"

"Uh…"

"Look, Tara, I'm simply interested in sharing some company for dinner. I eat enough meals alone to get tired of it. Stop worrying. I'm not going to pounce."

That was the second time he'd assured her on that score, but she was beginning to think it wasn't him pouncing she had to be concerned about.

"I'm sure you're not short on companions you could call on." She couldn't keep the cynical conjecture from her voice.

"You'd be surprised. I've never found the company of women with dollar signs in their eyes all that alluring."

She gave him a frank once-over. "Like women are only interested in you for your money."

"Is that a compliment?"

"Yes." She'd never been good at prevaricating. She hated lies, no more so than since she'd been lied to so spectacularly by Baron Randall.

"If you find me attractive, why not have dinner with me?"

"Because you are who you are and I am who I am."

"You mean the whole multimillionaire and junior-management trainee thing?" he asked with droll humor.

She found herself smiling. "Yes, that thing."

"Why don't we pretend to be nothing more than an unattached man looking for the company of a woman he admires a great deal for dinner?"

He admired her *a great deal*? That was a different line than Baron's had been anyway. He'd been so focused on her beauty and then her sexual innocence, he'd barely given credence to her brain.

"All right, but let's keep it simple. It's late."

"Do you have any suggestions?"

She did and couldn't help being surprised when he willingly let her direct him to a chain restaurant known for its quick and friendly service. The food was good, but not exactly five-star. Apparently, Angelo didn't care about eating only in the best restaurants.

She liked that and told him so.

He shrugged. "When you have the freedom and finances to eat where you want, why limit yourself? Besides, this was one of my dad's favorite restaurants when I was growing up."

"You grew up in the Pacific Northwest?"

"Seattle."

"Wow…I guess I thought all big business tycoons came from New York."

He laughed. "I have an apartment there. Does that shore up your image of me?"

"That depends…do you call it home?"

"I don't call anywhere home. I travel too much. I have a house in Palermo that would probably be the closest thing."

"Do you speak Italian?"

"Fluently."

"Oh…I took French in high school, but I was always more interested in numbers than languages."

"I'm fluent in several. It comes with the territory, but my mother spoke Italian to me always and we spent part of every year in Sicily with her family."

"You said she *was* Sicilian earlier…is she no longer alive?"

"She and my father died within two years of each other."

"I've heard about that kind of devotion…one can't go on living without the other." She'd always questioned it though…wondering if two people could ever really be that necessary to each other.

His face contorted as if in pain, but then went so blank she had to wonder if she'd imagined the first expression. "They loved each other very much."

He said it so coldly, as if he was unmoved by his parents' emotion.

Still…"Their deaths must have been very hard on you."

"I survived."

She nodded. He was too strong not to have done, but she wondered for just a second what the cost had been for him to be so detached about it now.

"My dad walked when I was two." Tara said after a silent pause. "He didn't know the meaning of the word devotion." Or commitment. Or love for that matter.

"Did your mother remarry?"

"Eventually. I had a few *uncles* who were every bit as allergic to the c-word as my dad before Darren Colby, my step-father, came into our lives."

"That doesn't sound like an ideal childhood."

"That's one way of putting it." She laughed, shocked at herself for sharing so much with a man she was determined not to get involved with.

The same thing had happened the night before. It bothered her, but a barrier that existed between her and the rest of the world seemed to be missing with him. Odd, but apparently it wasn't something she could do much about.

It was like her normal privacy filter was switched off around him.

Thank goodness he was only in Portland for a visit to his company and would be gone soon.

"Your mother must have had lousy taste in her partners," he said.

"That depends on how you look at it. She's drawn to dynamic, powerful men. Men a lot like you."

"For you to have had several male figures in your childhood, they must have been drawn to her, too."

"For a while anyway. She's beautiful."

"You say that like it's a curse."

"None of the men who dumped on my mom would have given her the time of day if she'd been plain."

"And perhaps Baron Randall would not have been attracted to you if you were not equally as beautiful?"

"I prefer not to talk about him."

"But he is the reason you are so reticent about becoming my friend."

"I never said that."

"Do you deny it?"

"No."

"And the man your mom married, Colby. I bet he was also attracted to her beauty."

"Darren would love Mom if she was fifty pounds overweight and had a mole on her chin."

"He sounds like a great guy, but wasn't he first attracted by her beauty?"

"I suppose."

"So, it isn't always a curse."

"No, but then there aren't that many men in the world like Darren."

"Maybe there are more than you think."

Did Angelo want her to believe he was one of them?

The prospect that he might was even scarier than her own urge to find out.

Over the next few days, Tara couldn't help feeling he was trying to convince her of that very thing.

Against her will, she found herself more and more attracted to the business tycoon who admired her brain and never criticized the fact she played down her beauty. He was charming to everyone, making Danette practically faint with excitement when he accepted an invitation to an informal barbecue at her place on Thursday night.

Under her brazen front, Danette was actually pretty shy and this would be the first major event she'd hosted at the condo her parents had insisted on helping her buy. Members of the city's elite, they had no problem providing their daughter with a home most people couldn't afford after working twenty years.

Even so, Danette had been worried about the success of her party and told Tara so. Having Angelo's attendance was a major coup, especially since so many other partygoers would be from Primo Tech.

"And don't you even think about trying to get out of coming now that you know he's going to be there," Danette said seconds after Angelo exited their work area.

"I told you I don't want to end up with another Baron Randall."

"Good gosh, Tara! Are you blind, or something? Not only is Angelo a good ten years younger than that swine, but the two men are so different they could be opposite species."

"Oh really? How are they so different?"

"First of all, it's no secret Baron Randall built his empire using other people."

A piece of information Tara wished she'd been privy to *before* meeting him.

"Angelo buys and salvages struggling companies. He's gotten where he is through the sweat of his own brow."

"Please."

"You know what I mean. He worked to build those companies up, just like he worked on this one. He's earned his tycoon status, not stolen it. And he's also not a womanizer."

"Oh, really?"

"Really. Ray did some checking for me at his newspaper. Angelo hasn't had a steady girlfriend in more than two years and he doesn't sleep with other men's wives."

"Like Ray could know that for certain."

"Angelo's newsworthy enough that if he had been caught with the same woman more than once it would have made at least one headline."

"The operative word being caught and one of the great benefits of being filthy rich is the ability to buy a newspaper's silence."

"Baron Randall is rich too, but there are still stories

about his womanizing ways in more than a few scandal sheets."

"Maybe he didn't care enough to have them squelched."

"What makes you think Angelo would?"

"Okay, so you've got a point. He's probably not a womanizer. Happy?"

"If you'll cut the guy some slack, yes."

She wasn't going there. "Is Ray going to be at the barbecue?"

"Sure. He's bringing his camera and taking pictures for my scrapbook." Danette smiled dreamily. "It isn't every day you get such a hunk of a multimillionaire in your backyard eating grilled steak."

Tara couldn't help laughing. "You are incorrigible."

Her friend grinned, her eyes filled with infectious laughter. "That's why you like me so much."

"So, are things serious between you and Ray?"

It had been her experience that when her friends started making cooing noises about settling down, they went into matchmaker mode with a vengeance and this barbecue invitation couldn't be seen as anything but.

Danette chewed on her bottom lip. "I think so. At least for me. He hasn't said anything about love, but he spends all his free time with me."

"That's a very good sign."

"I hope so."

And if it were true…what did that say about her and Angelo? They weren't dating, but he certainly managed to fill up most of her free time.

* * *

Thursday dawned bright and clear, the Oregon sun-shine for once unclouded by threats of rain. Tara walked to work from the light rail terminal with a smile on her face. It was a good day to be alive.

A strong masculine hand gripped her shoulder before she walked into the building. "You look happy."

She smiled up at Angelo, for once allowing herself to enjoy her body's reaction to the devastating man's presence. It wasn't as if anything could happen in front of the building in plain view of the parking lot and the rest of Primo Tech's employees. "I love the sunshine."

"It's a great day for your friend's barbecue."

"Yes, it is. Danette will be pleased."

"Speaking of, would you like me to pick you up on my way?"

"I don't…"

"I'd feel more comfortable arriving with someone."

"I don't see you as the shrinking violet type."

"I'm not." His expression said he couldn't imagine such a thing, either. "But I would still like to bring you with me."

They were both going and a car ride there and back could hardly do any damage. After all, she'd been in the car with him twice now and come away unscathed. "Sure, why not?"

His hand slid up her shoulder and cupped her nape, sending her thoughts skittering to the four winds. "I'll look forward to it."

She watched him walk away thinking maybe un-scathed was too strong a term to describe her living on the edge of going for another tycoon.

CHAPTER THREE

THE phone was ringing when Tara walked through the door of her apartment at twenty-five minutes after five. She sprinted across the small foyer and picked it up from the hall stand. "Hello?"

"Hey, hon…just wanted to make sure you're not going to dress like a bag lady now that the big boss is coming."

Danette.

"Sheesh…you called me to bug me about what I'm going to wear to your *casual* barbecue? Don't you have better things to do?"

"Right…it's casual and that means shorts and a T-shirt. Don't you dare show up in one of your casual-but-really-they-are-for-work-outfits."

Tara rolled her eyes. "What difference does it make?"

"Well, now that's an interesting question. It shouldn't make any difference…to you. I mean, if you're really not interested in the boss, then you shouldn't be bothered exposing a little flesh around him."

The idea of being around Angelo and wearing a pair of hip-hugging shorts and T-shirt that showed a glimpse of her stomach when she raised her arms made Tara's body flush with heat…and not from embarrassment.

"Come on," Danette added, "it's over eighty degrees outside. Be practical."

"I won't show up in a skirt and hose!"

"You'd better not and don't forget your swimsuit." Danette had sole use of the pool area at her condo complex to host her barbecue.

Tara loved the water, but if wearing shorts around Angelo made her jumpy, how would she deal with a swimsuit? "I'm not going to be swimming."

"Oh, please…did I mention it's eighty-some degrees out there? Of course if you get too hot and want to cool off, I could lend you one of mine."

Remembering her friend's penchant for string bikinis that showed more flesh than some bandages, Tara made a note to grab her own suit.

Just in case.

Angelo rang Tara's doorbell with more anticipation than he'd felt for a date in years.

Tara Peters was every bit as beautiful as her photos had shown, but she was also a very intriguing woman. He had no difficulty understanding Randall's fascination with her.

Angelo wanted her, too, which made this aspect of his revenge against the other man sweet indeed.

The door to her modest brownstone swung open and his breath suspended in his chest, all thought ceasing in a wave of shrieking male hunger that had him wanting to push her back into the apartment and claim her body as his own.

Denim shorts clung to her curves, stopping high enough on her thigh to make her well-toned, honey tanned legs look miles long. Her lemon-yellow T-shirt did some clinging of its own, revealing the fact her bra was so flimsy he could see her nipples peaking through the soft cotton.

Tara's arms came up and crossed over her breasts in a protective gesture that brought home to him the fact he'd been staring at her like a crass teenager watching a striptease.

Angelo's gaze traveled up to her face. She'd pulled her hair up into a ponytail. Still wearing no makeup. "You look about eighteen."

A damn sexy eighteen and he was glad he knew she was twenty-four or he would feel like a lecher with the thoughts going through his mind.

"And you *don't* look like a corporate magnate," she said smartly.

He leaned against the doorjamb, interested in the way she backed up a step as if his closeness bothered her. "Are you saying my business suits are all that stand between me and mediocrity?"

She laughed abruptly and shook her head. "You could never be an average guy. And I hate to tell you this, but most of the men at the barbecue are not going to be wearing Armani T-shirts and Ralph Lauren shorts."

His brows rose.

She grinned at him. "I used to be a fashion model. Identifying designers is my stock in trade. I can tell a knockoff designer bag a mile off."

"I'm not similarly gifted."

Her look said she doubted his words and he almost smiled. Men in his world often knew a great deal about women's fashion for the expedient reason that it made it easier to buy gifts a certain type of female would truly appreciate.

That sort of woman had never appealed to him.

"Are you ready to go?" he asked.

She nodded, grabbing her tote bag from the floor beside the door.

She waited for him to back up, but he merely shifted his body slightly so she could get by him. Tara gingerly stepped around him, as if afraid to touch him, but equally determined not to show it. He inhaled her scent, letting it tease his senses, before stepping back so she could shut the door.

Angelo's position forced her to stand mere inches from his body as she locked up. Then he led her outside to his car, where he took pains to invade her personal space buckling her in and adjusting her seatbelt. She was breathing in shallow pants, her eyes vague with suppressed desire by the time he straightened and shut her door. Good.

She wanted him and it wouldn't be long before he would have her—despite her aversion to wealthy tycoons.

The thought brought him harsh satisfaction. His revenge against the man who used and discarded people like trash was close at hand. However, unlike Baron Randall, once Angelo had Tara, he wasn't sure he'd let her go.

And that might be the best revenge of all.

"How many pictures do you need for your scrapbook?" Tara demanded of Danette as the woman's annoying boyfriend snapped yet another shot.

Angelo didn't like Ray's preoccupation with Tara, either, and was on the verge of making his displeasure known in a very basic way.

Danette shrugged her slim shoulders. "You can never have too many. And you've got to admit, even without makeup, you're awfully photogenic."

About that, Angelo had to agree.

But Tara grimaced. "I think I'm going to rue the day you took up your new scrapbook hobby."

"Hey, we aren't all so focused on work that we don't have outside interests."

"I have outside interests."

"Name one."

"I volunteer at the Boys and Girls club once a week."

That hadn't been in her file, Angelo took a mental note.

Danette snorted delicately. "Right, but you're doing almost the same thing at the club as you do at Primo Tech."

"Hardly."

"You manage staff resources. How is that different?"

"The staff is made up of volunteers."

Even Angelo could tell Tara was stretching the truth

and it made him smile. For a woman dedicated to work-life effectiveness, she was lousy at practicing what she preached. "So, you volunteer at the Boys and Girls club, but you don't connect with the kids?" he asked.

She turned to face him, her expression mirroring her surprise and some embarrassment. "I didn't realize you were there."

He handed her a cranberry spritzer over ice. "Your drink, as promised."

He'd been taking care of her in small ways like this one since they arrived at the barbecue and she didn't seem to know how to take it. Apparently other men in her life had not pampered her. However, he was intelligent enough to know that pampering and seduction went hand in hand.

She smiled, her rich chocolate eyes warm. "Thank you."

The snick of another picture came from her left and she jerked her head around. "Do you mind?"

Ray had the sense to look abashed. "Sorry. Photography is a fairly new hobby for me."

Tara sighed expressively. "You and Danette and your hobbies. Give it a rest, would you?"

"Sure."

Angelo gave the man a steely look that had sent more than one boardroom discussion going in the direction he wanted it to. "I wouldn't mind getting copies of some of the photos. Would that be possible?"

"You want pictures of the barbecue?" Tara asked, her voice pitched high in surprise.

"Not really, but there are one or two guests I wouldn't

mind having a photo of." He gave Tara a significant look.

"If you want a picture of me, I've got an entire port-
folio full I'm not using anymore." She said it like a joke,
but he didn't smile.

"I'd love to see them. Maybe you can get the portfo-
lio out when we get back to your place."

Her mouth opened, but nothing came out.

"If you can get her to show it to you, you'll be getting further than most of us. For a former top model, she
sure is shy," Ray said, sounding put out.

Danette smacked him in the arm, her eyes filled with
teasing laughter. "Hey, you are supposed be interested
in seeing my baby photos, not my best friend's modeling shots."

Ray grinned and shrugged.

Angelo frowned at him and the grin swiftly disappeared.

"Are you going to swim?" Danette asked Angelo,
going for a swift change of subject, apparently realizing he wasn't as amused by her boyfriend's interest in
Tara as she was.

The prospect of seeing Tara in a swimsuit sent his libido into overdrive. He met her wary brown gaze as he
answered Danette. "I'd like to."

"Good." She grinned at Tara. "How about you?"

"I don't think I will this time."

"Oh, come on." Danette waved her hand in front of her
face like a fan. "It's hot and I know you brought your suit."

"If you don't want to swim, we won't," he said making it clear he considered them a couple at this party and

had no intention of participating in activities that didn't include them both.

If anything, her expression turned more wary. "You don't have to refrain from swimming because I am."

"It's not a problem."

She gave the sparkling water a look of longing and he moved closer, until he could touch her shoulder.

Her head snapped up and their eyes locked.

"Are you sure you don't want to swim?"

"I…"

"What are you afraid of, Tara?"

She licked her lips and let out a short sigh before averting her gaze. "You."

He hadn't expected her honesty. "I promise not to dunk you."

"That's not what worries me and I think you know it." Tara spoke in a low voice so Danette and Ray, who were now arguing over when to start grilling the steaks, could not hear.

"A life worth living requires taking a few risks." Somehow, he was even closer than a moment ago.

"I've taken my share."

"Not with me."

"And you want me to believe you're different?"

"I am."

Tara's heart contracted at those two simple words. In a way, he'd already proven that. Other men would have tried to dismiss her reluctance to go swimming as trivial. Angelo saw the decision for what it was, an opportunity to either keep shutting him out or to let him one step closer to the private Tara Peters.

It represented a willingness to socialize with him, not only as a couple, but also in a situation that left her vulnerable. Few women looked their best with their hair hanging down their back in a wet rattail. And no woman put on a swimsuit in front of a man she was hugely attracted to without taking a risk.

Maybe after two years, taking this one small risk wouldn't be so bad. She might be inviting Angelo closer, but she wasn't going to bed with him. She wasn't offering to have his babies or buy his staff presents at Christmas.

"I'll swim."

He nodded, his expression every bit as serious as hers. "Okay."

Tara hadn't bothered with a wrap because her suit was pretty conservative, but as she walked toward Angelo, who watched her with blatant male appreciation, she wished she had. The navy-blue shorts and halter style suit covered almost as much as her clothes had, but it clung to her curves like a second skin and it was pretty obvious her sexy boss liked the view.

When she came within reach, he casually reached out and placed his hand on the bare flesh between her shoulder blades. "Nice suit."

Her breath caught and it took effort to force out a response. "Thanks. It's one of my favorites."

He guided her toward the poolside. "The body beneath it is fantastic."

She stiffened under his hand, the comment catching her off guard.

He gently increased the pressure and kept walking. "Don't tell me you aren't aware of how incredible your figure is. You've been a model for years."

"Was a model."

"Semantics shouldn't change your awareness of your own beauty."

"Beauty doesn't mean much in the scheme of life." And in her opinion, it often got in the way.

"Coupled with brains and a passionate nature, it's a pretty potent package."

Was he implying he saw her that way? "Few men care about what's under the surface."

"I'm unique."

"I get that you'd like me to believe that."

He didn't stop beside the pool, but kept walking, until he led her through a glass door into the building that housed half of the huge swimming pool. The condo complex was not only exclusive, its luxury amenities were without equal in the area. Residents could swim in whatever weather the Oregon skies chose to offer.

Danette had told Tara that was one of her favorite things about her new home.

Since the day was hot and sunny, no one else was availing themselves of the covered portion of the pool however. The illusion of total privacy heightened Tara's awareness of Angelo in a way she wished it didn't.

He paused on the edge of the empty water and looked down at her. The intensity of his gaze burned away her awareness of the sounds coming from the party outside. "You're not very trusting are you?"

"If I was after the way I grew up and what I went through with Baron, I'd be an idiot."

"You're far from stupid, but you're also blind."

She opened her mouth to argue, but he pressed his finger against her lips and she had to fight the urge to suck it into her mouth and taste his skin. "You can't see beyond your past. I am not from your past. I am right here, right now and I want you to see *me*."

She reached up and grabbed his wrist, the simple connection feeling too good, too *right* for comfort. She tugged his hand away, but kept her hold on his wrist and his fingers somehow went from pressing against her lips to cupping her cheek.

Her eyes locked with his. "I can't see anything else."

"Good." He leant down until his lips hovered just above hers. "That's the way it should be."

"You're awfully arrogant at times."

"I would bore you to death if I were any other way."

Was he right? Did she crave the same kind of man her mother had always been attracted to? Somewhere deep down inside she'd always known she did, which was why she'd shied away from men in general. She hadn't trusted her own judgment.

Could she now?

"I'm going to kiss you."

He waited, watching her with searing patience. He was giving her plenty of time to pull away, but right now that was beyond her. She wanted him, wanted his kiss. She needed to know if the feelings inside her were a figment of her imagination, or if connecting to this man would truly be as soul-altering as her senses were tell-ing her it would be.

Then he kissed her.

Carefully.

Slowly.

Thoroughly.

He didn't demand, didn't push for more. However, he still managed to take gentle possession of her mouth, imprinting his taste and the very essence of himself on her consciousness.

The almost soothing press of his lips against hers was not in the least aggressive and yet she felt completely, utterly claimed.

The expression in his eyes when he lifted his head said that as far as he was concerned, she had been.

"Are you ready to go swimming?"

The kiss had been so profound that the mundane question did not at first register. When it did, it also re-minded her that they were not really alone.

For a woman who hated having her personal life in the spotlight, she'd certainly given the other partygoers an eyeful.

However, on closer inspection, she realized that at the place they were standing inside the building, hardly anyone could see them even though the door that led outside was made of clear glass. Ray with his annoy-ing camera, seemed to be the only one even looking, the expression in his eyes smug.

Obviously he'd gotten a shot of the kiss. She won-dered if that picture was going to make it into Danette's scrapbook. Considering her friend's sense of humor, it probably would.

The pool looked more inviting than ever. "Yes. I'm definitely ready to get cooled off."

She realized the implication of her words as soon as Angelo's low chuckle reached her ears. Annoying heat surged into her cheeks. She'd blushed more around this man than she had since taking her first modeling contract more than ten years ago as a gangly adolescent.

"Then shall we go?" Angelo asked, tugging her toward the deep part near where it flowed to the outside, obviously intending to jump in.

She pulled back. "I'd rather enter at the shallow end."

He turned to look at her, his expression indecipherable. "Why?"

She shrugged. "I guess I'm the cautious sort, but I like to get used to the water a bit at a time."

"That's torturous."

He was right, but she'd never been able to force herself just to jump into cold water.

Something shifted in his penetrating blue gaze.

That was all the warning she got before Angelo swept her up in his arms and tossed her in the pool.

Cold water shocked her system. She sank toward the bottom, legs and arms flailing. Tucking her legs in, she executed a neat roll and shot toward the surface. It wasn't far, the pool was only six feet deep to begin with. She came to the surface gasping for air and ready to take an inch off his hide.

Impatiently brushing the water from her eyes, she

looked around, treading water and ready to yell at him, but he wasn't poolside anymore.

A sudden shower of cold droplets from behind her had her spinning around in the water. He was there, so darn tall, he could touch bottom and still keep most of his face above the water. He moved to her right, ending up not a foot from her in more shallow water. His expression was so relaxed and mischievous she couldn't begin to hold on to her anger.

She didn't think Angelo Gordon looked mischievous very often. Something spasmed in her heart that she was the one to bring out this side of him.

She sent a cascade of water directed at his head with the sweep of her hand. "You fiend." But her heart wasn't in it and the words came out sounding a lot more teasing than accusatory.

He grinned, not bothering to wipe the water from his face. "Feels good doesn't it?"

"It would have felt better if I'd been able to get used to it before being dunked."

He shook his head. "You would have wasted time playing in the shallows, torturing yourself with every small foray deeper into the pool."

"The shallows aren't always a waste of time."

"They are when diving into the deep end is so rewarding."

Neither of them was talking about swimming and from the seriousness of his expression now, they both knew it.

"I dove in once before and learned to rue my impetuousness."

"Which doesn't mean you should never go diving again."

"I almost drowned the last time."

He shook his head. "Not you. You got the breath knocked out of you, but you're fighting fit again."

He was right. Baron had hurt her, but her nature didn't allow for wallowing in misery. She'd picked up and moved on, in every way but her willingness to risk her heart again.

Angelo tapped her nose. "You're enjoying the water now, admit it."

"Yes, I am." What had felt frigidly cold against skin heated by the sun now felt refreshing.

"Diving into deep waters can be terrifying or rewarding depending on who you do your diving with and what kind of water he leads you into."

Oh, gosh. She didn't know if she could handle this. He'd been challenging her to see him as a unique individual since the moment they met, but this was more. This was a direct attack on the way she'd been handling relationships for two years.

Or rather avoiding them.

"What kind would I find myself in with you?" she couldn't help asking.

Strong fingers curled around her waist under the water and she found herself being pulled against him. "The kind that will leave you sated with pleasure."

"I've been sated before, but that didn't make up for the hurt that came later."

"No one can guarantee the future, *bella mia,* but the present is here for us to enjoy."

There was something extremely intimate about being called an endearment in his mother's native language. It made her feel special to him. Only that was probably wishful thinking. No doubt, he slipped into Italian with every woman he wanted to bed. It was sexy.

The cynical thoughts made her angry. Was she going to spend the rest of her life thinking the worst of every man who came into it? That made her a victim of her past, not victorious over it and Angelo had been right. She was a strong woman, too strong to let her past control her.

"Yes, the present is here for us to enjoy."

When his lips covered hers this time, there was no hesitation, no gentle persuasion. It was all raw passion and masculine claim-staking, a sensual demand that she acknowledge his ability and right to give her pleasure.

And she gave it to him through a mouth that willingly molded to his.

Lips cool from the water soon heated against hers and his tongue pressed against her mouth, this time demanding entrance. With a groan of needs long denied, she opened to him. Unlike Baron's carefully orchestrated seductions, Angelo took her mouth like a conquering marauder. Imprinting himself on every millimeter of the interior, he devastated her lips with a carnality that left her weak.

He lifted her more firmly against him, his reaction to their kiss pressing blatantly against her thighs.

Her breasts ached and swelled in the confines of her halter top, while her most secret flesh grew hot and wetter than the water surrounding them. She laid her hands against the sculpted muscles of his chest, her fingers delighting in the sensation of wet, slick skin covered by curling black hair. The kiss deepened into territory she'd never explored and she dug her nails into his pecs. He groaned against her lips.

A shower of water broke them apart, the sound of laughter around them grating on nerves sensitized by his lovemaking. And it had been lovemaking even if he hadn't done any more than kiss her. Some of the other partygoers had swum through the low arched partition to the outside and were engaging in a game of tag.

Incapable of the coordination it took to tread water, Tara took advantage of her proximity to the edge to grab it with both hands. She hung there while her body struggled for breath and she tried to regain control over her emotions.

"Do you want me to apologize?" He spoke very close to her ear.

She shook her head, not looking at him. "I was with you all the way."

"I didn't mean to lose control, *stellina*. Public displays of affection are not my thing. The thought of embarrassing a lover leaves me cold."

But then neither of them had expected the other guests in the pool to follow them inside.

"Stellina?" she asked, not ready to dwell on the implication of her own loss of control or his insinuation she was his lover.

His lips quirked. "Little star."

Thinking of her five-foot-nine stature, she shook her head. "Hardly that."

"It fits you."

"Maybe to a giant like you, but the rest of the world sees me as rather tall."

"How the rest of the world sees you is unimportant to me."

"Your arrogance is showing again."

"And we both know how you feel about that."

She turned away from the heat in his gaze. "I think your Sicilian blood is showing."

"Maybe a little, but don't chalk that kiss up to my Latin temperament."

"You want me to believe I'm wholly responsible for your passion? Isn't that giving me an awful lot of potential power?"

"Why should I attempt to hide what must be obvious?"

This was getting stranger by the second. Baron had always been careful to minimize the effect she had on him, or at least her impression of it. He had played control games, wanting her to believe the greater need was on her side. He'd spouted platitudes about love while withholding the security of knowing she impacted him with the same potency he did her.

Either Angelo was way more sensitive than Baron Randall or he was more confident. The latter was far more likely.

She turned her head and gave him a sideways look. "You're a unique man, Angelo Gordon."

"I'm glad you can see that." He waited a beat. "Finally."

No, no lack of confidence there.

A feminine hand landed on Angelo's shoulder. "You're it." The buxom brunette swam away at speed, her string bikini leaving nothing to the imagination.

To Tara's shock, Angelo joined in the game of water tag with enthusiasm and showed that he played shark in the water every bit as well as he did the boardroom.

CHAPTER FOUR

WHEN they climbed out of the pool forty minutes later to eat, Tara was panting from the exertion. She grabbed her towel and started drying off. He did the same.

She leaned over to wring her long hair out. "I wouldn't have pegged you for that kind of water play."

"What, you thought I only knew how to swim laps in a pool?"

"I would have thought water polo would be more your style—highly competitive and a definitive winner at the end of the day."

"Actually I was on a team through high school."

She straightened, surprised by the admission. "Were you really?"

"Yes, but the traveling schedule interfered with my studies and I dropped it my freshman year in college."

"I was right then."

He acknowledged it with a slight inclination of his head and then draped his towel around the back of his neck. "But I can also play a mean game of tag."

"Definitely." He'd tagged her several times, and unlike some of the men, made no attempt to cop a feel when doing so.

He really was different…from anyone she'd ever known. Even her stepfather…because as wonderful as Angelo was proving himself to be, she could sense he had a ruthless streak that would leave even a man of Darren's strength in the dust.

That ruthlessness was in evidence when they arrived back at her apartment later that evening. "Invite me inside."

"I don't think I should." She wasn't sure she was ready to take the next step in their relationship, or if she ever would be.

"Because of the kiss in the pool."

"Because of how much I want to repeat the experience."

He got out of the car and came around to her door. He opened it and leaned over her to unbuckle her seat belt. He stopped with his face inches from her own. "I won't continue to pay the price for another man's stupidity."

"You're so sure I don't want this because of what I went through with Baron."

"You do want this." His mouth claimed hers for another kiss that left any spoken denial useless. "You're afraid of me because of him."

"I told you about my mom."

"She had bad taste in men."

"Apparently so do I."

The chill in his eyes made her shiver. "I resent that remark. You want me."

"I didn't mean to imply you're a bad risk."

"But that's what you believe."

Frustrated anger welled up inside. "Are you saying you're interested in commitment? Marriage? That you'll stick around if a business opportunity comes up that makes our relationship impossible?"

"Most men marry someday and I don't do business in the bedroom so our relationship will never be compromised by my commercial interests."

"What do you want from me?"

"Invite me inside and we'll explore the possibilities."

"I don't believe in casual sex."

"There is nothing casual about where you fit into my life." The gravity of his expression and tone convinced her he was telling the truth.

As impossible as it might seem, this man was serious about her. He wasn't making any promises, but he wasn't denying the possibility of a future either. A very skilled seduction campaign or was he showing the marks of integrity she could rely on?

"If I invite you up, it isn't to share my bed."

"I'll settle for some coffee to start with."

"All right."

Angelo pulled back, shocking her by not cementing his victory with another kiss.

They had coffee and to her further surprise, he left around eleven without making a pass. Oh, he kissed her again and her lips were still tingling the next morning from it, but he hadn't tried to get her into bed.

Which had left her confused and unable to sleep for dwelling on the implications of everything that had happened at and after the barbecue.

* * *

She was yawning the next day when she sat down at her desk and looked over to see Danette doing the same thing.

They both laughed.

"Tired?" Tara asked.

"Yes, you look like you are, too, but I bet it's for different reasons."

"You're so bad."

"Well, admit it…you probably went home and worked on a project until bedtime, while I worked on Ray."

Tara laughed again, this time shaking her head. "You are incorrigible."

"And you aren't answering. Dare I hope you and the boss hit it off last night?"

"I'm sure Ray told you we kissed…I'd say it was pretty obvious we're attracted to each other."

"That doesn't mean a whole lot when it's you we're talking about. You've got more fortitude than anyone I've ever known."

"Are you saying I'm stubborn?"

"If the conservative shoe fits…"

Tara just shrugged, not wanting to get into a long discussion about her date with Angelo and knowing that was where this conversation was headed if she didn't watch it.

She and Danette worked for a while before her friend piped up with, "Ray thinks you two are a great couple."

"Ray needs to spend more time focusing on you than what's going on around him. I was ready to throw his camera in the pool last night."

Danette gave a gasp of mock horror and clutched at

her heart. "He paid a thousand bucks for that baby. He would have cried like a lost orphan if you'd drowned it."

"I guess it's a good thing your hobbies feed each other."

The phone rang before Danette could reply to Tara's teasing.

She picked it up. "Tara Peters here."

"Good morning, *stellina*."

"Angelo." She turned so her back was to Danette's now avidly curious gaze.

"Did you sleep well?"

"If I answer that honestly, you'll get a swelled head." Where the flirtatious words came from, she didn't know.

She'd never been particularly flirtatious and in the last two years, she'd been positively subdued in her behavior toward men, but he brought out a side to her she'd considered gone forever.

"I did not sleep." The words were given in such a seductive voice, she about melted in her chair.

"Um…I'm sorry?"

A wicked chuckle made her insides shiver. "I'm not sure I believe you."

"You doubt my sincerity?"

"Perhaps I wouldn't if you answered my original question…did *you* sleep well?"

"No."

"Ah. I like that. It was because of me."

"Conceited man."

"Am I?"

"Maybe not." She had spent her night thinking about him.

"I need to be back in New York on Monday."

"Oh." Gosh, how original, but what was she supposed to say to that? *Don't go?*

"My flight was scheduled to leave this afternoon."

"It was?" As in he'd changed it?

"Yes."

She waited in silence, not sure how he wanted her to respond. Hoping she'd interpreted his use of the past tense correctly.

"I had it postponed."

Relief surged through her and she knew she was in deep trouble with this man. "You did?"

"I wanted to spend more time with you."

"I like *that*," she admitted.

"So, you'll let me take you out tonight?"

"Yes." She was making an irrevocable decision, but maybe it was time she started taking some risks.

If she didn't, she might spend the rest of her life regretting yet another bad choice.

"I'll pick you up at seven."

"All right."

"You have a date with the boss?" Danette demanded the minute Tara hung up the phone.

"Yes."

Danette's whistle echoed the shock reverberating through her own brain.

She was still reeling from her decision to actually go on a date with Angelo when she dressed for the evening.

Unlike their business dinner, she had no desire to dress in a way that downplayed her femininity tonight. Pulling a garment she hadn't worn in a very long time from the back of her closet, she smiled. The quintessential little black dress, its spaghetti straps and skirt that hit her midthigh were elegant and sexy despite the simplicity of the dress's design.

She brushed her hair into curling waves that reached the middle of her back, slipped on a pair of black stiletto sandals and stood to look in the mirror. Oh gosh, she'd forgotten the way it looked. The way she could look.

Had it always been this sensual? Half of her body was on display and the neckline showed a lot more cleavage than she remembered.

Even without makeup, the woman staring back at her appeared ready for a very hot date and she wasn't sure that was the image she wanted to provide. Angelo didn't need a whole lot of encouragement in this area. She was reaching for the zipper on the back of the dress when the doorbell rang.

He was early.

She looked longingly at the less revealing dresses hanging in her closet and started to jerk the zipper down when the doorbell rang again. She pulled the zipper back up and after giving her reflection one last despairing glance, she headed for the door.

When she opened it, she almost fell backward from the intense appreciation in his gaze. He looked like he wanted to eat her alive. Zings of forbidden pleasure arced through her at the thought.

Taking a deep breath, she tried to ignore the incredible reaction of her body to his presence. "Hi."

"Hello." He looked her up and down, his fiery gaze touching her with tactile force and leaving goosebumps in unimaginable places in its wake. "I like the way you look."

"Thank you."

He'd changed from a business suit to a v-necked, lightweight, black sweater that molded his muscular chest and charcoal gray slacks that emphasized the sheer masculine perfection of his form. "You don't look so bad yourself."

His smile was more like a wicked invitation to sin. He put his hand out. "Ready to go?"

"I don't have any makeup on yet." Not that she normally wore it, but this was a date.

Not counting yesterday, which had not been official…it was her first one in two years.

"You don't need it."

She cocked her head to the side and studied him like he was an alien species. Sometimes, like now, it felt like he was. He certainly didn't fit the mold of the other males she'd known. "Most men want their dates to be as gorgeous as possible."

"You aren't an ornament on my arm. You look beautiful to me and that is all that should matter."

"Thank you."

"Besides, makeup cannot improve on perfection." It was a corny line, but he said it was such offhand seriousness; she couldn't dismiss it as mere flattery.

"Wow…you know just the right thing to say."

"The truth often comes out that way."

"But not always. Sometimes the truth hurts." She didn't know why she said it, maybe as a reminder to herself.

His mouth set in a grim line. "You're right, but I still prefer it over dishonesty."

"Me, too." A sudden urge made her blurt out. "Promise you'll always tell me the truth."

He stared at her as if testing her motive for the request, but then he nodded. "I won't ever lie to you."

"I'll never lie to you either." She said it quietly, fervently and he received it without comment.

Taking her arm, he tugged her out the door. "Now that we've established that, let's go eat dinner."

She laughed, a feeling of buoyant happiness bubbling through her. Unless he was the best actor on the planet, he'd meant his vow of honesty and she knew she had. No matter how odd the pact might seem to others, it gave her a sense of peace and a spark of hope for their future.

They were in Washington Park before she thought to ask where he was taking her for dinner.

"We're almost there."

To her knowledge, there was no restaurant near where they were, unless you counted the concession stands in the Rose Garden. Which seemed to be where they were headed, but she couldn't imagine he was taking her there.

She saw that she was right about their destination however as he pulled the purring Mercedes into a parking spot near the gardens. He came around to open her door and the scent of roses washed over her senses. Midsummer, the air was laden with their sweet fragrance.

She closed her eyes and inhaled. "It's what I think Heaven will smell like. So sweet and good."

"I'm glad you like it."

He helped her out of the car and then led her through an archway and down into the gardens. He kept going until they reached one of the private gardens enclosed by a tall green hedge. He stopped and she saw a linen covered table set with china and lit with candlelight in the center of the small garden bedecked with a thousand more flickering candles. Two antique dining chairs were on opposite sides of the smallish table and he seated her in one before taking the other.

A black clad waiter immediately poured them each a glass of champagne and then set starters of chilled crabmeat over a bed of lettuce.

She looked at Angelo, too stunned to pretend to be the least bit casual about his efforts. *"This is amazing."*

"I wanted tonight to be special."

"Any particular reason?"

"Because what is going on between us is special."

His words seduced her utterly.

Dinner was an incredible experience. They talked about everything including Angelo's plans for Primo Tech. He listened to her ideas on the subject and then brought up two more companies he was currently resuscitating.

That discussion took them all the way to dessert when Angelo said, "Tell me about Baron Randall."

Her muscles tensed. "I already did."

"Only some of it."

"Do you spend your other dates quizzing women on past liaisons?"

"Only when those liaisons are still impacting the present."

"He doesn't. I'm here aren't I?"

"He does. You're here against your better judgment. Because of your experience with him, you wanted to write me off."

"I've been writing *all* men off for two years. It's not personal."

"It became personal the moment I got lumped in with the rest." And in his arrogant view of the world, that was unacceptable.

She almost smiled.

"Your refusal to date makes it sound like you're not over him." He didn't sound pleased at that idea.

"I am, trust me."

She couldn't read his expression, but she wasn't sure he believed her.

"I told you I wouldn't lie to you."

"But if you are lying to yourself, how will you help it?"

"I'm not that much of a fool."

"I hope that is true."

She wasn't offended by his words. In fact, their urgency touched her. "Trust me. It is."

"How did you meet?"

"At a show." Perhaps talking about it would set Angelo's mind at rest. Goodness knew she felt more comfortable sharing her secrets with him than anyone else, though she still wasn't sure why. "He asked for an introduction from my agent and then swept my then naïve self right off my feet."

"He's quite a bit older than you."

"Sixteen years and that was a big part of his success where other men had failed. Not only did he know just what buttons to push to get a response from me because of his experience, but I made the mistake of assuming age meant maturity. That he knew what he wanted."

"Didn't he?"

"Yes, I guess he did…but in the end, it wasn't me."

"So you broke up."

"Yes."

"He married an heiress within a month of the break-up."

"Don't ask me how he accomplished that. She had to have heard the stories. We were splashed across every newspaper. Why would she want a man who had to have been having an affair when they met?"

"He was living with someone else when he met you."

"How did you know that?" She hadn't even learned that juicy tidbit until she read one of the nasty articles done on their breakup.

He shrugged. "I read."

"Well, I didn't know about her until later."

"I see."

"I doubt it."

"You sound bitter."

"The tabloids slayed me…portrayed me as the skirt

on the side while Baron had been courting his one true love. They dubbed me *Tempting Tara* when I was the one who'd been tempted and then tossed aside."

"Anyone who knows Baron Randall would know that he's absolutely incapable of having one true love."

"You know him?"

"We've met." The cold dismissal in his voice left no doubt what Angelo thought of the other man.

"So, you don't think I'm some sort of floozy, ripe for the picking by another charismatic tycoon?"

"Floozy?"

"You know what I mean."

"Yes, I do and no, I don't."

"But—"

"I want you. That's not a crime."

"No."

"So you think I'm charismatic?"

"On occasion, yes."

"That's good to know."

"I'm sure you think so."

"If it means I get the girl, I do."

"The jury is still out on that one."

"Then let's see if I can't rig it."

"What?"

He was standing up and his hand was outstretched. "Come for a walk with me and let me turn some of this charisma on you."

He was teasing, but it wasn't a joke. The man was way too attractive for Tara's own good. And as docile as any lamb, she still put her hand in his and let him lead her toward the main part of the rose garden—that had been closed off for their enjoyment alone. Its lush beauty in the fading light awed her.

"It's incredible here," she said after several minutes of silence.

"I think so, too. It's one of my favorite places."

"Did you visit when you lived in Seattle or discover it when you bought Primo Tech?"

"When I was a kid, we came every summer. It was like a pilgrimage."

And he was sharing this special place and his precious memories with her. That meant something. It had to.

"My mother loved the Rose Festival and we drove down for it," he continued, "I liked the rides."

"I can't imagine you on a carnival ride."

"I was a little boy. Even tycoons had to be children at some point."

"It's hard to picture. I see you trading companies from your crib."

"Actually I didn't get interested in the business side of things until I was twenty. Before that, I thought I would be an engineer like my father had been."

"What changed your mind?"

"Life." He put his arm around her waist and pulled her into his hard, warm body. "My father was technically brilliant. He developed several new designs and started his own company."

"I'm surprised he was a success. A lot of engineer types aren't good when it comes to the day to day operations." She'd seen it over and over again at Primo Tech.

"He wasn't the greatest businessman, but he made do."

"Whereas you are brilliant business wise."

"And a mediocre engineer."

"There are always trade-offs in life."

"Yes, there are."

"What's the name of your father's company?"

"It doesn't exist anymore. It was absorbed into a bigger company."

That surprised her. "I would have thought you would keep it intact. A pride thing."

"I didn't own it at the time."

"I'm sorry." She sensed that caused him a lot of pain.

He turned to face her. "Let's not talk about business right now."

"What do you want to talk about?"

His head lowered. "This," he said as his lips pressed against hers.

It was unlike any of the other kisses had been. This was both tender *and* passion driven. Desire vibrated off of him and against her mouth, but he didn't push for a deeper kiss. When he was done, he lifted his head. "You are so sexy, *stellina*."

"You make me want to be."

Triumph rippled through Angelo. For two years this woman had wanted to be anything but sexy. She had avoided men and intimacy completely, but in his arms, she wanted to be a woman.

She was so close to being his—he could sense it.

"Come on, there is something I want you to see."

She let him guide her toward the lower part of the rose garden. He kept his hand on her shoulder, his thumb brushing her nape. Triumph flared through him when she shivered despite the warmth of the air and shifted toward him infinitesimally.

Experience had taught him that often it was the small touches which seduced a woman, not a blatant show of passion. She already knew how much he wanted her. He'd shown her that in the pool. Now he had to show her it was okay to want him too…because he knew what to do with her wanting.

He leaned down so his breath caressed her ear when he spoke. "I know how to satisfy your craving to be a sensual woman, Tara. It will be very, very good between us."

"I…" Her voice trailed off as if she didn't know how to respond to his comments.

He wasn't so reticent. "I will give you more pleasure than you have ever known. Believe it."

This time it was a full blown shudder that rippled down her spine. *"Angelo."*

He was not even kissing her, but already her arousal was making her voice husky and her heartbeat quicken. He smiled. She didn't know it, but they had just passed first base on their way to a home run.

CHAPTER FIVE

By THE time they returned to the car, Tara was a mass of throbbing sensation.

Angelo and she had lingered in the garden for quite a while. He had shared a surprising knowledge of the different species of roses, having her smell them and feel the softness of their petals as he explained their differences.

All the while, he had been touching her and saying things in that husky, deep voice of his that promised the sun, the moon and the stars all wrapped up in one ultra masculine package.

As battle strategies went, it had been extremely effective. He'd vanquished her resistance and moved her toward surrender with the speed and efficiency of a well-armed, seasoned campaigner. It was the recognition of her comparative lack of experience that made her hesitate to give total surrender.

Could she really be sure of what she wanted and what was best for her when she was under the influence of his charismatic presence? When her hands were literally shaking with the need to touch him?

She turned toward him as his car slid into a parking spot in front of her brownstone and was struck anew by his sheer masculine perfection. So sexy. So strong. So much a man. She wanted him more than she'd ever wanted anyone, including Baron.

Which made it all the more imperative that she not dive into an emotional commitment without knowing where he was at in that regard.

She could remember all too clearly the times she had said she loved Baron and gotten no response or an, "I know." She could see now that he'd only said the words to her when it suited his strategy for manipulation.

She no longer had such naïve illusions about love, but sex wasn't a simple slaking of physical needs for her, either. It never could be. She needed to know that more than Angelo's hormones were engaged. She wasn't giving her body to another man without being sure he saw her as more than an occasional bed partner.

Angelo switched off the ignition.

"I'm not going to ask you up."

He tensed and turned to face her, his jaw set, surprise making his eyes darken. "Why not?"

Time for total honesty. She sensed any attempt at prevarication would only give him the final leverage he needed to bring about her surrender. "Because if I do, we'll make love and I'm not ready to do that yet."

He reached out and cupped the back of her head, his thumb tracing the shell of her ear and making her tremble even more. "You want me."

No way could she deny it. "Desire isn't enough."

"What *is* enough?"

She stared at him, nonplussed by the question. She hadn't expected him to want to discuss the intricacies of a relationship. Most men shied away from that sort of thing.

But, goodness knew, Angelo Gordon was unlike any other man of her acquaintance. "I don't want to be treated like a one night stand."

Which was as far as she'd gotten in her thought process…or as far as she had allowed herself to go.

"I want more than one night."

"How much more?"

"How much more *do you want?*"

"I'm not sure."

"That's not good enough."

"I can't quantify it."

"Sure you can. What do you want? Protestations of love?"

She, who no longer believed in love, felt her heart rate double at the mention of the word. Was he saying he was falling in love with her? How could he be?

"What do you want, Tara? A promise of fidelity, or do you want more?" he went on relentlessly. "Perhaps an offer of marriage. Is that what you need to feel good about giving yourself to me? Commitment with a capital C?"

Was he saying he would give those things to her, or was he testing her, pushing to figure out the parameters of the deal?

"I just realized I wanted to pursue a relationship," she said, frustration at being put so firmly on the spot lacing her voice. "How am I supposed to know what form

I need it to take before I'm ready to be intimate with you?"

"You're too smart not to know your own mind."

Only right now, her mind was muddled by desire and the need to conquer fear. She doubted he ever got muddled in his thinking. Probably, he thought he was being extremely reasonable asking her to define what she needed, but he wasn't the one with doubts. Somehow, she couldn't see this man ever being the one with the doubts.

Her only defense against his relentless logic was more honesty. "Look, you were right, Angelo. I have been letting my past control my present. I don't want to do that anymore, but that doesn't mean I'm ready to jump into bed with you. I need time."

His smile was all sensual, predatory, and it confused her, because it wasn't the expression of a man who had just been turned down. "Oh, you're ready all right, but you're hesitating because you don't know where it will lead."

She throbbed low in her womb and she knew he was right. "Fine. You're right. There aren't a lot of options for where sex between us could go."

"This is always true. Those options do not change over time."

"Some of them become less palatable."

"You do not want a one night stand, but I gather you also don't want a few long weekends with us both moving on to other partners?"

The mere idea made her shiver with revulsion. She'd never taken sex casually and the idea of going into a relationship that intimate with the expectation of ending it repelled her. "No."

"That leaves two other outcomes…we move in together—"

"No," she practically shouted.

His brow raised in question.

She took a deep breath and let it out. "I stupidly went that route once before…even after watching my mom make the same mistake over and over again. I won't be controlled by my past, but I won't refuse to learn from it, either."

"Then there is only one alternative left: marriage."

"I—"

"You see, it was not so hard to define. In order to give yourself to me, you want a lifetime commitment."

"I'm not angling for marriage." But her words came out a mere whisper of sound, the direction the conversation had taken shocking her to the core.

"Aren't you?"

"No." She wasn't, darn it. Frustration welled up in her. "If you weren't trying to go so fast, this wouldn't even be an issue, so don't try putting all the blame back on me. I only said I'm not keen on having casual sex with a man who will disappear from my life very soon."

"I wasn't aware I was trying to blame you for anything and I agree, casual sex is not what I had in mind."

A maelstrom of emotion churned through her. *"We can't get married just because you want to have sex with me."*

"People do it all the time actually, but I think we've got a lot more than sexual desire going for us."

"Let me get this straight," she said, feeling more bewildered than she ever had in her life. "Are you saying *you want to marry me?*"

"Yes."

Suddenly she felt claustrophobic in the interior of the car. She couldn't get enough air and the world was going black around the edges. "You didn't say that," she breathed.

"I don't just want you, I like you, Tara. It's been a long time since I felt that way about a woman. I'm thirty years old and I've never been in love. I don't think I'm wired that way. There are a lot worse things I could do than marry a woman I want as much as I want you."

She couldn't think of a single thing to say in response. Baron had put off making any major commitments with a constant stream of excuses. So had her mother's boyfriends. She'd never known a man like Angelo that wanted to jump feet first into long-term commitment…except Darren.

Her stepdad had asked her mom to marry him on their second date. But that was because he loved her and Angelo had just said he wasn't wired that way. It didn't make any sense.

He sighed at her silence. "I respect your integrity and your intelligence. I enjoy your company and I think you feel the same way about me. You probably thought you loved Baron Randall, but look at where that got you. Marriage to me would be a lot better for your emotional well-being than waiting around for another man like him to show up."

"If you feel that way about it, we can keep dating… take our time deciding if a future makes sense."

Something came over his expression, the ruthlessness she'd always been sure lurked under his civilized exterior.

He shook his head decisively. "Some of the best decisions I've made in my life have been spur of the moment based on my gut instincts. Those instincts are telling me that a marriage between us would work."

This was beyond anything she could've imagined.

"So, what? You want to fly to Las Vegas and get married tomorrow?" she asked sarcastically, trying to point out the ridiculousness of his attitude.

"That would work," he said musingly. "I think I could wait one more night to have you."

"You're insane."

"Not even close. I'm merely sure of what I want."

She shoved her car door open, feeling as if she didn't get out of that car immediately, she was going to lose it. "I need to think."

"You sure you won't ask me up? I could work on convincing you."

"No!" She clambered from the car. "I don't think that's a good idea."

He didn't appear worried by her rejection. In fact, he gave her another look filled with sensual confidence. "I'll be by to take you to breakfast. We'll spend the day together."

She nodded and reeled like a drunk up the walk and into her building. Luckily someone had left the front door unlatched because keys would have been beyond her right after she got out of the car.

She wasn't much better when she reached her door on the top floor. The phone was ringing when she got it unlatched.

She rushed inside and picked it up, still feeling dazed. "Hello."

"*Stellina*. I wanted to make sure you made it inside all right."

"Yes, I'm here." Which was definitely an exercise in the obvious, but scintillating, even intelligent conversation was beyond her.

"I do not like the fact your building has only one locked exterior door and I noticed it was left open. It is old…even locked, it could easily be broken into."

"This isn't New York, Angelo."

"Bad things happen here, too."

"I'm fine."

"Yes, but I'll be glad when we're married and I can know you are always safe."

She tried her best not to dwell on his use of the word *when* instead of *if*. "You mean if I married you, I could look forward to your hiring me a bodyguard?"

"That's an idea worth considering. I have plenty to go around."

She was still gasping with indignation and leftover shock when he said goodbye and hung up the phone.

Surprisingly she slept well and woke up feeling refreshed before the alarm went off.

The phone rang as she was getting out of the shower. It was Angelo telling her he wanted to take her to the beach and to dress appropriately. He also suggested she bring spare clothes in case they got wet or sandy. She couldn't help wondering if he didn't have plans to try to stay overnight, but she found herself packing the clothes and other necessities anyway.

Was she engineering her own downfall? His proposal had fried her brain cells.

Angelo parked his car in a spot near the entrance to the beach. Despite the warmth of the day and it being a Saturday, the spot was deserted. It was the reason he favored this beach over others and why he'd built a vacation home not far away. He liked the solitude.

He'd take Tara to his house later, when her initial reticence to being alone with him had diminished.

They got out of the car and stopped in unison to take stock of the view before them.

"It's gorgeous," Tara breathed, her voice filled with awe.

Blue water stretched out as far as the eye could see and waves crashed against huge, mountain like rocks jutting out of the water a couple hundred feet from the shore.

"Yes." He looked down at her. "But the view isn't the only beautiful thing around here."

She averted her face, but he could see his compliment had pleased her. Once again, she'd gone for a very feminine look, wearing a cropped tank top and low rider shorts that showed lots of leg and the smooth skin of her stomach. Her sandals were strappy bits of nothing that accented the delicate lines of her feet.

She'd pulled her thick chestnut hair up into a youthful ponytail again, leaving the slender column of her neck exposed.

He leaned forward and placed a warm, lingering kiss against the sensitive spot behind one ear. He inhaled her fresh, sweet fragrance and nuzzled her. "You smell good."

"Thanks." She pulled away with a jerky, nervous movement. "We'd better get down to the beach."

"We're not on a timeline." But he let her lead him away.

He could afford to wait to solidify his advantage. He had no doubts about how this day would ultimately end. And he was enjoying the wait.

They walked down a path from the parking lot to the beach. As soon as they hit the sand, Tara stopped and pulled her sandals off. She let them drop behind a log near the path entrance.

"Are you sure they'll be safe there?"

"Do you see anyone around to steal them?"

There was only one other car in the small parking area and the only other occupants of the beach were nothing but small dots in the distance. "Point taken."

"You should take off your shoes, too."

He hadn't walked barefoot on the beach since he was a kid, but there was something about an untamed beach and sunshine that brought out even a tycoon's need to connect more closely to the elements. He slid his sports shoes and socks off and left them next to Tara's sandals.

Then he put his hand out and she took it. They walked hand in hand to the shoreline, their silence surprisingly companionable considering the heavy subjects they had been discussing when they parted the night before.

The sand was warm against his feet, but the heat generated from their palms pressed together was greater. He got a primitive charge out of touching Tara in any way. Even the slightest connection sent electric impulses along his nerve endings and knowing that making her his took her away from his enemy gave him an equal charge.

He hadn't been nearly as surprised by his proposal as she had been, but then he knew what lengths he was willing to go to get his revenge against the man who had destroyed the grief-stricken and vulnerable woman who had given Angelo his life.

Marriage would be a much more effective tool in removing the possibility of reconciliation between Randall and Tara than mere seduction.

"How seriously do you take the commitment of marriage?" Her words told him her thoughts had been going along the same course as his own.

"It's the ultimate commitment between a man and a woman."

"Do you consider divorce an easy out if things get difficult?"

"No."

She stopped and looked up at him, her brown eyes questioning. "What do you really think about marriage?"

"I want a companion."

"There's more to life than bed." Their thoughts had been traveling along *very* similar paths.

"I said a companion, not a bed warmer. I like talking business with you. It's stimulating."

She grinned, a naughty gleam in her dark eyes. "I've never had my opinions described that way before."

"They're that, too," he said, easily sliding into the game. "You're the first woman to turn me on while talking about the merits of on-site employee day care."

She laughed, the sound warm and inviting. "What else?"

"Children. I want a family. I've built an empire I have no desire to leave it to some hospital who will build a wing with my name on it." As he said the words, he realized how true they were.

Why not Tara as the mother to his children?

He certainly had no illusion about falling madly in love and living happily ever after with some dream woman. And he'd be destroying his enemy in the process.

She nodded, looking thoughtful. "So you see marriage as pretty much permanent."

"Don't you?"

"Yes. The worst part about growing up was the upheaval every time one of Mom's boyfriends left. I won't put my children through it. I want a marriage that is going to last."

"Ditto."

She smiled at that, but didn't say anything else and they walked along the shoreline for several minutes, the call of seagulls and the surf the only sounds around them.

Then she stopped abruptly and leaned down to pick up a red bucket some child must have left behind. She looked at it as if the bright plastic somehow held the answers of the universe.

She turned and tugged his hand. "Come on."

"Where?"

"I want to build a sand castle." She led him to the spot where the sand was still wet but no longer brushed by waves from the outgoing tide.

Stunned, he just stared at her when she plopped down to her knees and started scooping damp sand into the bucket.

She peeked up at him, her eyes wide behind her sunglasses. "Are you going to help?"

"Why?"

"Why help or why build?"

"Why build?"

She shrugged. "I've always wanted to build one and I never have."

"Never?"

"I grew up in the Midwest. I didn't even see the ocean until I started taking modeling jobs that required travel. I moved to Portland for Primo Tech, but I've spent most of my life living in land-bound states."

If someone had told him that seducing a former model included building a sand castle, he would have dismissed the idea as nonsense.

"Come on," she cajoled, "don't be a spoil sport. If you can build companies, you can build one small sand castle."

It didn't turn out that small. She wanted turrets and a moat, as well as a courtyard and a castle that any royal family would be proud to live in.

It took them two hours to complete. When they were done, she sat back on her haunches and surveyed their handiwork with satisfaction. "Very nice."

"It looks formidable."

"Like a princess could live protected behind its walls all the days of her life." A strange expression shot through her brown eyes. "But it's only sand. Just like most fantasies in life, it looks great, but it won't survive the incoming tide."

"Not all dreams disappear when tested by reality."

"Most of mine have."

"What kind of dreams?"

"Oh, I don't know. I was going to grow up and be a supermodel."

"You were very successful."

"But no Cindy Crawford."

"Why would you want to be anyone else?"

She laughed at that. "It's a girl thing."

"What other dreams got washed away on an outbound tide?"

She sighed and then sat back on her already sand covered bottom, her gaze fixed on the castle. "When I was a little girl, I dreamed of having a family. By the time Darren came along, I no longer trusted the dream." She fiddled with one of the sticks they'd discarded as too crooked to stand atop the turrets as a flagpole. "I'd moved out before I accepted he wasn't going to."

"But he didn't."

"No. He stayed with Mom, but then I made the mistake of dreaming of my own future with a man I loved. It took almost two years, but eventually I realized that whole Prince Charming fantasy was just that. It was no more real than this." She pointed to the molded turrets and empty moat.

"What exactly are you saying?" Did she want to avoid marriage altogether?

Now that he'd decided it would be the best form of revenge and that marrying her wouldn't exactly be a hardship, he would not accept a refusal.

She looked at him then, her dark gaze intense. "I'm not looking for love and a perfect happily ever after anymore."

"And yet you are hesitant to marry me. Why?"

"I need to know that what we have is more than a sand castle on the beach."

"How many years was Darren your stepfather before you moved out?"

"Six."

"You spent six years wondering if he was real…you could spend just as long wondering about me, but I am real and so is my proposal."

Then he did what he was best at and kissed her slightly parted lips.

Angelo's mouth took possession of hers as he dragged Tara into his lap.

And that fast, she was lost. It all felt so incredibly right. The heat of his body against hers, his uniquely masculine scent surrounding her and the spicy warmth of his mouth both comforted and enticed her. The feel of his rock hard muscles holding her gave her a primitive sense of security no modern woman would admit to.

As much as her mind told her attraction to this man spelled danger in capital letters, her body responded to his as if she'd found the other half of her whole. The half she hadn't known was missing until this very moment.

She wanted to dismiss such thoughts as juvenile and fanciful, but they permeated her being with rock solid staying power. Her *soul* knew this man.

Hard, mobile lips molded hers perfectly and with just the right amount of pressure that she moaned under the onslaught to her senses.

He growled in response to the sound, his hand gripping her waist tightly. She felt like she was being kissed by a wild predator claiming his mate, not a refined businessman. She responded on a level she had never allowed herself to explore before, digging her fingertips into his shoulders and reveling in the leashed power she sensed there.

He lifted her by the waist, repositioning her so she straddled his hips and their torsos were pressed close together. She could feel the threat of his hardness against her most sensitive flesh and the layers of clothes between them did nothing to negate the heat that connection generated.

Jolts of sensual awareness rippled through her body, making her arch toward him and shudder while his lips continued to entice her passion to greater heights.

Suddenly his thumb brushed upward from where his big hand rested against the indentation of her waist. It caressed her in an up and down motion, teasing at her rib cage just below her breasts before dipping down over the curve of her hip.

Her breath suspended in her chest as she waited for him to explore further, to actually touch swollen flesh chafing at the restrictions of her bra. But he didn't and she found herself breaking her lips from his to suck in much needed oxygen.

"Angelo," she panted.

She didn't know what else she wanted to say, couldn't form a cohesive thought to save her life.

His hands curved around her in a hold so possessive, she gasped. "This thing between us is good. Don't dismiss it, *stellina*."

She had no answer, so she remained silent.

He kissed her temple and then the corner of her mouth as if he couldn't help himself before guiding them both to their feet. She dusted the sand from her clothes and her legs, while he pulled something small from his pocket.

It was a mini digital camera. He aimed and took a shot of their sand castle, then took a picture of her looking at him.

She wasn't smiling. She had no idea how she looked. Her thoughts were deep and her body was still vibrating with sensual awareness.

"You wanted a picture of our sand castle?" she asked, surprised by the gesture.

"There is more than one way to preserve a dream."

The message in his eyes was one she was terrified of interpreting so she turned away.

He laughed, the sound husky, as she started back up the beach. "I won't let you run from me, Tara."

She didn't answer because if she was honest with herself, she'd have to admit she didn't want to.

CHAPTER SIX

TARA wasn't exactly shocked when Angelo pulled his luxury car into a spot in front of a Frank Lloyd Wright style house positioned on a cliff overlooking a private beach not far from where they'd built their sand castle.

She'd half expected him to offer to rent a hotel room so they could shower the sand off before dinner, but the privacy and subtle magnificence of the home was beyond anything she would have envisioned.

"Is this yours?" she asked as he turned off the car.

"Yes."

"I'm surprised you keep it considering how little time you must have for vacations."

"I've found it useful in hosting negotiations with West Coast companies."

Ah. That made sense. Seclusion and the home court advantage…both great assets to have on his side when working on a business deal.

The inside reflected the stark simplicity of Wright architecture, but the quality of both the house's furnishings and minimalist décor pointed to Angelo's wealth.

An Important Message from the Editors

Dear Reader,

If you'd enjoy reading romance novels with larger print that's easier on your eyes, let us send you TWO FREE HARLEQUIN PRESENTS® NOVELS in our LARGER PRINT EDITION. These books are complete and unabridged, but the type is set about 20% bigger to make it easier to read. Look inside for an actual-size sample.

By the way, you'll also get a surprise gift with your two free books!

Pam Powers

Peel off Seal and Place Inside...

84

THE RIGHT WOMAN

she'd thought she was fine. It took Daniel's words and Brooke's question to make her realize she was far from a full recovery.

She'd made a start with her sister's help and she intended to go forward now. Sarah felt as if she'd been living in a darkened room and some- one had suddenly opened a door, letting in the fresh air and sunshine. She could feel its warmth slowly seeping into the coldest part of her. The feeling was liberating. She realized it was only a small step and she had a long way to go, but she was ready to face life again with Serena and her family behind her.

All too soon, they were saying goodbye and Sarah experienced a moment of sadness for all the years she and Serena had missed. But they had each other now and that's what

She held

Printed in the U.S.A.
Publisher acknowledges the copyright holder of the excerpt from this individual work as follows:
THE RIGHT WOMAN Copyright © 2004 by Linda Warren. All rights reserved.
® and ™ are trademarks owned and used by the trademark owner and/or its licensee.

YOURS FREE!
You'll get a great mystery gift with
your two free larger print books!

GET TWO FREE
LARGER PRINT
BOOKS!

YES! Please send me two
free Harlequin Presents® novels
in the larger print edition, and
my free mystery gift, too. I
understand that I am under no
obligation to purchase
anything, as explained on the
back of this insert.

PLACE
FREE GIFTS
SEAL
HERE

106 HDL EFY5   306 HDL EFZH

FIRST NAME   LAST NAME

ADDRESS

APT.#   CITY

STATE/PROV.   ZIP/POSTAL CODE

Are you a current Harlequin Presents® subscriber and
want to receive the larger print edition?
Call 1-800-221-5011 today!

(H-PLPP-03/06) © 2004 Harlequin Enterprises Ltd.

The Harlequin Reader Service™ — Here's How It Works:

Accepting your 2 free Harlequin Presents® larger print books and gift places you under no obligation to buy anything. You may keep the books and gift and return the shipping statement marked "cancel." If you do not cancel, about a month later we'll send you 6 additional Harlequin Presents larger print books and bill you just $4.05 each in the U.S., or $4.72 each in Canada, plus 25¢ shipping & handling per book and applicable taxes if any.* That's the complete price and — compared to cover prices of $4.75 each in the U.S. and $5.50 each in Canada — it's quite a bargain! You may cancel at any time, but if you choose to continue, every month we'll send you 6 more books, which you may either purchase at the discount price or return to us and cancel your subscription.

*Terms and prices subject to change without notice. Sales tax applicable in N.Y. Canadian residents will be charged applicable provincial taxes and GST.

He led her to a bedroom with a huge plate glass window that overlooked the ocean. "You can shower and change in here."

"Thank you."

She watched him walk away, her feelings no more settled than they had been on the beach.

After her shower, she brushed her hair out in front of the mirror in the large en suite bathroom. She left it down, shimmering in silky waves over her shoulders, contrasting against her white dress. She'd thought this dress was more conservative than the one she'd worn the night before even though it also had spaghetti straps.

It fell to her ankles in a form fitting line that was nevertheless not clingy. However, the row of tiny buttons that began at the sweetheart neckline stopped eight inches above the hem, leaving a slit that parted when she walked. And it struck her that a man of Angelo's temperament would see the buttons as some kind of challenge.

She bit her lip, wishing she'd brought something less in your face feminine.

Just then, he walked into the room. The lack of a warning knock said more about his sense of possessiveness than it did his lack of manners. She had a feeling the oversight had been very deliberate.

"Ready?" he asked, dressed in a pair of dark chinos and white Polo shirt that set off his dark skin while accentuating the sculpted muscles of his chest.

Talk about sexy.

She put her hands out in a stock modeling pose. "What do you think; am I ready?"

His eyes flared with blue heat as he gazed at her. "You look beautiful."

"Thank you." She slipped her feet into a pair of heels. "Now, I'm ready to go."

He put his arm out and she took it, saying nothing when he casually suggested she leave her things in the room for later.

She was curious to see what his plans for the night were. After his comments before they left the beach and the way she had responded to him, she wondered if he was considering using sexual intimacy to convince her of their compatibility.

She'd made the mistake once of believing great sex meant a great relationship. She wasn't that naïve anymore, but she couldn't deny the surge of sexual awareness she had every time he was near, either. Even Baron had not impacted her so startlingly with his mere presence.

Dinner was fabulous and she couldn't help thinking about how Angelo had told her that he enjoyed her company. She liked being with him, too.

As much as she wanted him, it wasn't all about sex.

Though that was what was primarily on her mind in the confines of the car as he drove them back to the beach house.

"It's late. Do you want to spend the night?" he asked as he pulled into the parking spot he'd used earlier.

"Wasn't that your plan all along?" Her tone wavered somewhere between censorious and teasing.

He shrugged. "It occurred to me, but if you aren't comfortable, we'll drive back to Portland tonight."

At least he was being honest.

"There are multiple bedrooms," she said, knowing even as she made the remark that the likelihood of more than one being used was very small.

"Yes."

"We'll probably end up in the same one, though."

"That is entirely up to you."

And her libido, which was as out of control as it had ever been in her life. Even so, she didn't want to spend what remained of the night in the car driving home and then seeing him off at her front door.

She wasn't sure what she did want, but saying goodbye to him was not it.

"It makes the most sense to stay."

"Excellent." He opened his door and swung his legs out of the car. "I wasn't looking forward to driving back across the mountains this late."

But he would have done it if she asked him to. That was worth something. Her trust was gently building without her really realizing it.

He built a fire in the great room's fireplace and opened the sliding glass door that led to outside. The sound of crashing surf filled the room and cold air rushed in to make the heat from the fire welcome, even though it was summer. Not atypically on the Oregon coast, it had started getting chilly the moment the sun went down.

She slipped her heels off and stretched her toes in the plush carpet before moving to stand near the floor to ceiling window beside the open door. She loved summer because of the long days and gorgeous sunsets.

This one was almost over, but it had been spectacular. The deep red and orange reflected off the water as the light faded. She didn't know how long she stood there, how long Angelo let her simply watch out the window, but the sky faded to a deep purple and then there was nothing but black night out the window. Soon, the moon would be out, but for now, the darkness made it seem as if they were alone in the universe.

It gave her a strange feeling, one she needed to counteract, and fast.

She remembered spying a familiar game case on one of the built-in shelves. "Do you fancy a round of Backgammon?" she asked without looking to see where he was.

There was nothing but silence behind her.

She turned to see why he hadn't answered and ran smack into his chest.

He cupped her shoulders and looked down at her, his expression doing impossible things to her insides. "I want *you,* Tara."

"So, you do plan to try to convince me with seduction." She couldn't quite decipher the change in his expression and that made her nervous, bringing out the cynicism she'd used so many times in the past to hide behind. "Or is it the other way around? Are you hoping your proposal will smooth the way for getting me into bed? And then maybe tomorrow, or the next day, or whenever you get ready to move on, you start making noises about how maybe we aren't really all that compatible."

Her tone was nothing short of an accusation, her

words deliberately offensive, but he didn't get angry. In fact, he didn't tense at all. He simply looked at her like he knew something she didn't, something really important. Something she wanted to know but was afraid of finding out.

His mouth came down and hovered just above hers.

"You—" a barely there kiss against her lips "—are—" his tongue flicked out to taste the corner of her mouth "—going to—" another kiss, this one more firm "—to have—" again his tongue…this time exploring the seam of her lips "—to trust—" his hands landed on her hips and pulled her into intimate contact "—me."

He tilted his pelvis toward her, leaving little doubt of the level of his arousal. Then, another kiss, this one demanding entry to her mouth while his hands rotated her hips against him. How could being pressed into such intimate contact with such blatant male sexuality feel so natural, so right?

Just like on the beach, her body reacted to his nearness as if it had found its sole home in the universe. She had no defense against something so profound.

She parted her lips on a sigh of surrender she prayed she would not regret.

His tongue took possession of the heated interior of her mouth and increased the temperature several degrees. He tasted so good, better than the slice of banana split cheesecake he'd cajoled her into having for dessert. Her arms snaked around his neck and she went up on tiptoe to duel with his tongue in an ancient dance of erotic desire.

The world tilted and she realized she was being carried. She didn't know where and didn't much care. She was too busy trying to devour a pair of sexy, masculine lips that she thought she just might be content to lock with for the rest of eternity.

He stopped moving, bent slightly and then no light filtered through her eyelids. Even that reality couldn't hold her attention for very long, but when he laid her down on the plush carpet, pulling his mouth from hers, her eyes flew open and she moaned in protest.

They were in front of the fire, its orange glow the only light remaining in the room. It flickered over his features like a magical ebb and flow of illumination and shadow. She lay on her back staring up at him, her heart beating wildly while her lips pulsed with the need for more of his kisses.

He came down beside her, propping himself up on his elbow. So close their bodies touched, his leg slightly covered hers, and his chest pressed against her arm.

She felt surrounded by him, completely closed in, and her breaths came in shallow pants.

"Afraid?" he asked, not sounding particularly concerned.

"You said I should trust you."

His dark brow rose, the firelight lending a primal cast to his face. "Do you?"

"I'm working on it."

He smiled one of his rare smiles. "Good."

She said nothing and he brushed her face with his fingertips, leaving a trail of tingling sensation in their wake. "You are so beautiful."

Those words had been said so many times to her over

the years, they'd almost ceased to have meaning. However, he was not seeing her as a body prepared to show some designer's creation off to advantage. He was looking at her as a lover and no man had been allowed to do that in two long years.

Even before, Baron's appreciation of her beauty had been wrapped up in his own pride of ownership. Something she had never been comfortable with, no matter how much she had thought she loved him.

Angelo looked at her as a man looked at a woman he could not look away from, not a woman he desired to show off to others.

The words unfurled inside her with a burst of pleasure and she savored them in silence for several seconds before replying. "Thank you." She brought her hand up to trace the chiseled features of his face and down his neck to his collarbone. "You are a beautiful man."

The corner of his lips quirked in amusement. "I've never thought of myself in those terms."

"Most men don't." She grinned, feeling ridiculously happy for no reason she could discern. "However, you can trust me on this. Aesthetically you are extremely pleasing. Feature for feature you have the most masculine beauty I have ever seen. And I saw a lot of beautiful men in my former profession."

"So, you think I'm the sexiest guy you've ever met?"
"Yes."

"It's those Sicilian genes." The smug arrogance in his voice was more amusing than annoying.

She laughed. "Both of your parents must have been devastatingly attractive people."

"I suppose."

"Don't you know?"

A dark shadow crossed his features and his mouth flattened into a grim line. "Yes, but it isn't something I've thought about in a long time."

"You don't like talking about them, do you?"

"No."

"Maybe it would help whatever bothers you so much if you did." She was no amateur psychologist, but she couldn't help feeling he kept too much of himself hidden.

Said the pot to the kettle.

She almost sighed, but bit it back. She wasn't any better than him, but she had told him more about Baron than she'd even told her mother. And she felt better for it.

He traced the neckline of her dress, allowing his finger to dip into her cleavage for a breathless second. It felt amazing, just that small touch, but she sensed they were on the verge of something more important and she willed herself not to get sidetracked by how good it felt to be next to him.

"Angelo?"

"It's too private."

"Even to share with the woman you want to marry?"

An arrested expression came over his features and his gaze shifted from her breasts to her eyes. "You want me to talk about them to you?"

"Yes."

"It's important to you?"

"I think it is."

He sat up, looping his arms around one raised knee and ran his fingers through his hair. "I don't know where to begin."

"Wherever you want." She scooted into a sitting position beside him, glad for the warmth of the fire now that he wasn't touching her.

Her nipples peaked from the cold air blowing in through the open doorway. She didn't want it closed however. The sound of the surf was soothing.

"My dad met my mom when he was in Sicily negotiating a contract." Angelo's voice was void of emotion…no remembered pleasure, no residual pain, nothing. "He fell for her like a ton of bricks within minutes of their meeting. At least that's how he used to tell it. He went after her as only a brash young man sure of what he wants can do."

"You wouldn't know anything about that," she teased.

He shrugged, not even cracking a smile at the small joke. "It's not the same. This was love—the kind you hear about in fairy tales I guess."

Something clenched inside her at his words.

He'd fallen silent, maybe sensing her inner turmoil.

"Go on," she urged.

"Dad talked Mama into marrying him and returning to the states with him."

"That sounds pretty romantic," she had to admit. She might not believe in love and happily ever after for herself, but it sounded like his parents had certainly known what that was all about. "Were they happy?"

Pain spasmed across his face and laced his voice

when he spoke. "Yes. They were deeply in love for all the years of their marriage, but Dad died of a heart attack when I was twenty. Mama was lost without him."

"I'm sorry."

"I was, too. She didn't know how to run a company and I was still in school. I wasn't ready to take over the reins."

"That would have been hard for you."

"Even harder when I realized what that had cost us."

"What did she do?"

"She hired someone, a man who came highly recommended. He was brilliant and seemed to really know his business. *I liked him.* I worked alongside him at the company during my summer break that year. I thought he was teaching me the ropes so I could take over as soon as I graduated." Self-disgust dripped from Angelo's words.

"Is he the one responsible for you losing your family company?" she asked with an awful premonition.

"Yes."

"Because he wasn't as good as you thought?"

"Because he was a lying, using bastard who did whatever it took to get what he wanted."

"That doesn't sound good."

"He seduced my mother into selling him the company at half its worth and then dumped her."

The words hung in the air with poison still capable of causing pain. Tara could feel it. *She* hurt.

This guy had been worse than Baron. She shuddered at the thought. She hadn't thought they got any slimier.

"He was ten years her junior, but it didn't matter,"

Angelo went on, his voice flat now. "She was so grief stricken, she was easy prey for him and all the while I thought he was being a good friend to her while I was away at school."

"You blame yourself."

"Not as much as I blame him."

"So, he just walked away from her after he got his hands on your company?"

"Not before destroying my mother. He mocked her for believing a man a decade younger would want to marry her. He ruined her sense of honor and woman-hood." His fist hit the floor. "I thought he was my friend, but when I found out he'd been screwing my mother, I wanted to kill him."

"You didn't."

"I might have. I was angry enough and there are a lot of primitive urges passed down by my Sicilian ancestors, but I was too busy dealing with her suicide."

Horror clawed through her heart and she felt nausea well up inside. "She killed herself. Over him?"

"She still loved my dad when this monster came into her life. He used her loneliness against her and when it was over, she felt she'd betrayed Dad's memory. She came from a very traditional Sicilian home and she couldn't face what she'd done."

"Did she tell you this?"

"She left a note…wanted to explain to me so I wouldn't hate her. God knows I never hated her, but she couldn't live with herself…with the memories, the hu-miliation and hell, probably the loneliness."

"So she gave up?" At least her mom had kept fight-

ing. No matter how many mistakes in judgment she made about men, she'd never given up and abandoned Tara.

"He killed her." The words came out like bullets and she knew Angelo believed them implicitly.

Tara didn't say anything. In a sense he was right, but in her opinion, his mother had let him down, too. Women got hurt all the time by men they trusted. Just look at her own mom…and her own past. His mom's choice had been cruelly selfish toward her son, but Tara couldn't condemn her…had no interest in doing so.

She saw immediately that Angelo's belief he wasn't wired for the more tender emotions came from a bone deep determination never to be at risk to them like his mother had been. His steely determination was palpable.

"Thank you for telling me."

He looked at her coldly. "No more questions? You don't want to know how she died or what happened to the bastard who used her so mercilessly?"

"Only if you want to tell me."

"She took pills. They'd been prescribed by her doctor to help with the grief after Dad's death. She went to sleep curled around his pillow and never woke up again."

"I'm so sorry." It was inadequate, but she didn't know what else to say.

Some things were just too big for mere words.

"It's been ten years."

"And it still eats at you."

"But not for much longer."

"You plan on getting revenge against the guy who did it?"

His gaze became shuttered. "You know me well. Yes."

Somehow, she wasn't surprised he'd waited so many years to get the guy back. Angelo was a heck of a businessman and that meant he left nothing undone. Any revenge plot he devised would have every angle covered.

"You're Sicilian. It's in your nature," she tried to say lightly, but it came off flat and she sighed, "I hope it gives you the satisfaction and closure you need."

Angelo's jaw could have been hewn from granite. "It will."

She bit back an argument. Vengeance wasn't going to bring his mother back or restore his family company to him, but maybe it would allow Angelo to move on. She was surprisingly unconcerned by the fact the man who wanted to marry her was caught up in a revenge plot.

A dedicated businessman, she was sure he'd choose that avenue for retribution. His empire was built on saving failing companies and she didn't see him destroying an empire and all of its employees to crush a single man. More likely, he'd take it over. And considering what kind of man Angelo would be taking it from, she had no trouble thinking the unscrupulous toad deserved it.

Then Angelo turned toward her and the sensual predator was back gleaming at her from those indigo eyes.

She sucked in a breath at the swift change. "Angelo?"

"Old grief has no place in our present, *stellina*."

She would have replied but he was pressing her back to the carpet, his lips applying pressure to hers, while sexual intensity rolled off of him in palpable waves. It was so overwhelming, she was shocked by the gentle way his mouth explored hers.

She could not imagine what kind of training he had gone through to learn this kind of self-control, but it awed her.

So did his sexual expertise. She thought she'd known all there was to know from a man experienced in the art of seduction, but Baron didn't have a patch on Angelo.

He built her desire with caresses that touched everywhere and lingered nowhere. The fire crackled in the hearth beside them, the wind blew in the scent of the ocean to wash over their heated bodies and every nerve ending she possessed came to life with stunning power. Surge after surge of electric desire rushed through her until she panted and shook with need.

He palmed her breast, his big hand engulfing the swollen flesh. Her nipple, already beaded, now ached with the need for more stimulation. Only, the careful pressure of his hand muted by the layers of her top and bra was not enough. She arched up into his hand anyway, striving to increase the friction.

He rotated his palm. Sensation shot from her nipple straight to the core of her and she pressed upward, moaning.

"I want to touch your skin," he whispered in an erotic growl.

"*Yes.*"

He unbuttoned her bodice, one small button at a time. He paused between each one to place a baby kiss on the skin revealed.

"Oh, Angelo…" Her fingers scrabbled in the carpet beneath, vainly trying to find purchase—something to anchor herself to with the storm of emotions raging through.

"This is a very sexy dress, sweetheart." He spoke against her chest, the hot air from his mouth making her shiver in a response as far removed from being cold as possible.

"Thank you."

"You may wear it again."

She laughed at the sheer arrogance of his statement, the sound strangled.

Finally, he peeled the front of her bodice away from her body to reveal her white lace bra that conveniently hooked in the front. Had she worn this particular bra and panty set on purpose? Had she subconsciously hoped he would do exactly what he was doing, which was un-latching the bra with one-handed dexterity she couldn't hope to emulate?

He took his time peeling back the bra cups, using each movement of the fabric to increase her arousal, while teasing her with what was to come.

Oh, gosh…this man knew exactly how to touch her.

He looked down at her naked torso framed by the white fabric of her dress with blatant male appreciation burning his gaze. *"Bellisima, cara."*

"You sound so sexy when you speak Italian," she said on a sigh. "What are you saying?"

"Most beautiful. And you are that, Tara."

He hadn't translated the *cara,* but even she knew what that meant. Darling. Was she darling to him?

She hoped so because the more time she spent with Angelo Gordon, the more she felt for him.

His fingertip traced circles on her breasts, first one and then the other...back and forth...first left...then right...but never touching the hard nubs that ached for his attention.

"Please, Angelo."

"What do you want, *cara?* Tell me." His voice was thick with passion, the subtle Italian accent coming out.

"I need you to touch me."

"I am touching you."

"More. I need more."

"What more?"

"You know."

"Perhaps I do, but just to be sure, I want to hear you say it."

"No." Suddenly she felt all too vulnerable. He was wringing a response from her that was greater than anything she'd ever known. "Don't make me say the words."

He lifted his hand away from her and met her gaze square on. "Why not?"

She had to suck in air before she could speak. "It gives you all the power."

"No, it does not. Whatever you ask for, I will give. That puts the power directly in your corner."

"You won't make me beg?"

A feral grin slashed across his gorgeous face. "Only if you want me to."

And he was just the man that could make her want such a thing.

"How could you possibly know I want you to?" Even Angelo was no mind reader.

"You won't ask directly for something. You'll say words like *more* and *please* and make me guess what more it is you want." His voice was every bit as devastating as his touch—so rich and smooth and full of erotic promise.

"So, anything I ask for you will give me?"

"Anything."

Baron had never given her that kind of power in bed. She couldn't think of any other man who would. It took a tremendous amount of confidence and consideration to make the offer.

"Even if I ask you to stop?" she pressed.

"Especially if you ask me to stop."

He really was putting the control in her hands. No man had ever done such a thing. He might seduce her body, but he wanted her to give permission with her mind before he did it. It was such a tantalizing concept, she shuddered in renewed need.

"I want you to touch my nipples." Heat that had nothing to do with sexual arousal flooded her cheeks, but excitement at saying the words out loud also coursed through her body.

"Your wish is my command." He rotated his fingertip on the very tip of her hardened peak.

Excitement crashed over her in wave after wave of incredible pleasure, but it still wasn't enough.

"Harder, please." Then remembering what he'd said, she husked, "Pinch it."

He did, gently and then more firmly and she couldn't

help the soft animalistic sounds rasping out between her parted lips. He tortured her with soft then firm touches until the sensitive flesh throbbed with aching intensity and her breath was coming out in hitched little gasps. Then he moved to her other breast and did the same thing while her head thrashed back and forth on the plush carpet.

"You look like a sensual fantasy in the firelight."

The words shocked her, so lost was she to her feelings. "I feel like a woman on the verge of ecstasy," she breathed out.

His hand moved to the remaining buttons on her dress and started undoing them with the same enticing kisses between each button until her lace panties were revealed. He stopped then and brushed across the front of the lace and she jumped from the sensation.

He smiled. "Nice. They match your bra."

"Yes." Was that her voice—so husky it was practically a whisper?

He finished unbuttoning the dress, baring her completely to him but for the scrap of lace covering the heart of her.

Her legs parted of their own volition from the heat of his gaze.

He took the silent invitation with a speed that made her cry out as his fingers slid between the lace and her skin to dip into the warmth of her feminine center. His mouth moved down her body until it closed over one distended nipple and this time her cry was so harsh it made her throat ache.

He sucked and she whimpered.

His fingers did magical things to her sensitive flesh. She started gyrating against them, her hands gripping the back of his head and keeping him pressed to her breast in frenzied strength. A tension she hadn't known in two years built and built until it broke over her like a tsunami wave.

There was no way she could contain it and she bucked against Angelo, crying out his name and demanding more with an abandon she had never felt before.

He kept up the nerve-racking touches until her body jerked with each light caress and shook from an overdose of pleasure.

She grabbed his wrist. "Stop!" she begged.

He did, cupping her with possessive tenderness that made her eyes sting.

CHAPTER SEVEN

SHE didn't know how long they lay together like that before it occurred to her what she had just experienced had been very one-sided. And he hadn't said a thing…had not demanded entry to her body or anything!

What kind of amazing man was he? Certainly, he was unlike any other she had known or heard about.

She reached down with the hand closest to him and brushed the back of her fingers along the rigid length of his erection.

A low sound of pleasure rumbled in his chest. "Mmm…that feels good, *cara*."

"Do you want to make love, Angelo?"

"We are already making love, but if you are asking if I want to have intercourse…" He paused and she waited with bated breath for him to go on.

"Without a doubt, I want you, but I promised you. No seduction. After what just happened between us, it could be nothing but."

He was right, but… "Maybe I've changed my mind… maybe I want to be seduced."

"I don't break my word, Tara." Despite the obvious arousal of his body, his tone was absolutely firm.

She respected that. A lot. Only that didn't mean he had to lay here like a statue in sexual agony.

She brushed her hand back and forth, loving the way his big body jerked from the small caresses. "I c…could please you in other ways."

Angelo's only response was a very primitive growl deep in his throat. Taking it as acquiescence, she turned on her side, pleased with the way he kept his protective and highly erotic hold on the apex of her thighs. It felt like they were connected intimately.

She undid his trousers and slipped her hand inside. He was big and hard against the silk of his boxers, tenting the fabric significantly. She gulped at the thought of making love completely, but sensed he would never hurt her, not this man who had been so careful to keep his word even when she tempted him not to.

She caressed him and he went even more rigid.

She reluctantly pulled his hand away from her and sat up to kneel beside him. She grabbed the waistband of his trousers.

He rolled onto his knees and then stood so she could slide his trousers down and then the boxers, taking care not to catch his hard length on the waistband.

Her breath expelled from her lungs in a long whoosh at the sight of his hard flesh so close to her face. "You're um…very prepared."

He chuckled. "I've never heard it put that way before."

She leaned forward, but he reared back. "Please

don't. If you put your mouth on me, my good intentions are going to take a vacation and not come back until I'm buried deeply inside you."

She nodded her understanding and stood. She let her dress slide from her body completely.

His eyes glowed his appreciation.

She smiled. "I want you to take off your shirt, too."

"Hot?"

"You don't know how much."

She choked on a laugh before joining him on the carpet, this time with him on his back and her snuggled up beside him.

"That feels good."

"I haven't done anything."

"You don't have to. Just having your body beside mine is a turn-on."

No beautiful Italian speech there, but she appreciated the sentiment and curled her fingers around him in reward. "Amazing. You're so soft."

"Soft?" he choked out.

"I mean your skin…like silky velvet. Can there be such a thing?"

"If you say it is, I believe you. Right now, I would believe anything you want me to."

She laughed. "I doubt it, but you just keep saying stuff like that."

He didn't laugh. He moaned as she started stroking him. She listened to the hitches in his breathing pattern to determine how he liked to be touched. It was the most incredible experience she'd ever had, having this powerful man put himself at her mercy.

"Tara…"

"Yes, *cara,* yes! *Don't stop.*"

She didn't and he erupted with a masculine shout that rang in her ears. Her body went stiff against him as if sharing an echo of his ecstasy. She'd never felt anything like it and collapsed against his side as if she'd found her own completion.

Eventually, they snuggled in front of the fire for a long time before he got up and carried her into the bedroom. As she had suspected, they ended up sharing a bed.

Tara saw Angelo off at the airport with the promise to have an answer to his proposal by the following weekend.

She couldn't believe she was making him wait, even harder to believe he was letting her.

He'd made it clear he wanted her decision now, but he hadn't pushed for it. It had to be obvious she wanted him enough to risk pretty much anything…even marriage. But he had agreed to wait for her decision and that made her feel really good.

Baron had always insisted on having his own way, so had most of the men her mother had lived with.

Angelo wasn't like that. He wanted her compliance sure, but not at the cost of her self-respect and that meant the world.

Not wanting to make the same mistake with Angelo, she had with Baron, she spent a good portion of her off-hours that week researching him. Everything she found, which wasn't much…the man was very private, pointed to him being the opposite of Baron.

He was absolutely ruthless when taking over a company and making it profitable, but he was also known for his ability to turn all a company's assets to a profit, including its current workforce. He gave regularly to charities, was honest as far as she could tell, and as Ray had told Danette, Angelo was not a playboy.

In fact, there was almost nothing that she could find about him in the social columns. He didn't have much of a personal reputation at all.

Everything she could find on him was related to his almost supernatural ability to make money and turn a dying company into something great.

She'd searched for information on his father's company, but without knowing its name, she'd had no luck. And its loss was never referred to in the articles written about him now. Except for what he'd told her, his past was shrouded in mystery.

His present was filled with business, but his life was not littered with people he'd used and discarded once he'd gotten what he wanted from them.

The turnover rate in his corporate headquarters was very low. Another good sign, if she needed one. He was a trustworthy man.

Thursday evening, she stood in the grocery checkout line, tiredly waiting for her turn. It had been a long day, an even longer week. She'd missed Angelo more than she'd thought possible. How could someone become so necessary in such a short time? She'd lain awake every night wrestling with her inexplicable desire to acquiesce to his marriage proposal. It made no sense and yet, her heart told her she needed the man.

She didn't trust that organ, but found its promptings impossible to ignore…thus her sleep deprived exhaustion.

She yawned behind her hand while the checkout clerk argued with the man in front of her over the sale price on a can of chili. Someone had to be sent to verify the price listed on the shelf.

Knowing that nothing was going to happen until the matter had been resolved, she let her gaze roam over the magazines and weeklies displayed at the check stand. Her eyes skimmed the headlines, noticing two Elvis sightings and one alien baby claim before she was arrested by a picture that looked like…no it couldn't be.

But it was.

A full color image of Angelo kissing her in an obviously heated embrace in Danette's pool filled the front of one of the weekly tabloids. The headline read, *Tempting Tara Takes Another Rich Lover…*

Would she never be rid of that awful nickname? Darn it, she wasn't the one who had done the tempting in her relationship with Baron, or the one with Angelo for that matter.

The tag line under the photo was worse. *Will going to bed with the boss put this former model on the fast track to success in corporate America?*

She grabbed the tabloid with a jerk that almost tore its front cover and yanked it open. She flipped the pages with angry flicks until she found the article. It was a two page spread with more pictures. Lots of them. Every one insinuated sexual intimacy between her and Angelo.

One showed them coming out of their hotel room at the coast. Angelo's arm was around her, his body language and expression possessive. The implication was unmistakable, but the editorial copy spelled it out anyway.

Like two years before, she was painted as a money-grubbing whore, only this time with her eye to the main chance at Primo Tech. An unnamed source in the management training department was quoted as saying it looked like Tara was hoping to gain her promotions via an avenue even older than hard work and perseverance.

It was all there…her affair with Baron, further speculation on her being the other woman when he courted his oil heiress. There was even some nonsense about how he'd been keeping her under surveillance since the breakup and innuendo that she might be at fault for the rumored possibility of imminent divorce.

Tara's stomach somersaulted and it took a full minute of shallow breathing before she was sure she wouldn't lose what little she'd eaten that day. She'd skipped lunch, trying to get ahead at work so she could take a half day off on Friday and keep her weekend free. Angelo was due in early the following afternoon.

Had he seen the article? She had no way of knowing. Surprisingly he had not called her all week. She had expected him to at least attempt to sway her decision with frequent phone calls, but he hadn't. She only knew when he was due back because he'd told her before leaving when to expect him.

Her gaze re-focused on the article. *How many people had seen it?*

The weekly didn't have the highest circulation in the country, but it was a national publication.

She couldn't believe this was happening all over again and it made her furious. She hadn't done anything wrong, but she was being painted as a scheming tramp who used her body to get ahead instead of relying on her brains. That made Tara angriest of all. She'd graduated at the top of her class and was darn good at her job. She didn't need the company owner's *patronage* to get a promotion.

She was perfectly capable of securing one on her own merits, thank you very much.

The whole situation would be ludicrous if it didn't hurt like a knife to the gut. Twisting that knife was the knowledge that whoever had sold the picture and information to the tabloid had been at Danette's party. And one of her co-workers had been willing to be quoted, if anonymously, saying something extremely nasty. Betrayal burned through her.

She didn't know who she worked with that felt that way, but only one person had gone around taking picture after picture at the party. Ray…the budding journalist.

He'd told her he was a *serious* journalist and that photography was only his hobby. The weekly was hardly an impressive example of journalistic solemnity and those photos had been paid for, which made the little hobby *a job*.

An ugly, despicable job…but one that could not be denied. Her stomach cramped again as an even less palatable thought assailed her. Had Danette known about it?

Two years ago, a couple of models that Tara had thought were friends had betrayed her to the press. One going so far as to tell out and out lies about her, exacerbating the piranha like media frenzy feeding off of her misfortune. That had hurt almost as much as Baron's rejection.

So, maybe Tara was being hopelessly naïve now, but she simply could not accept that Danette had been in on Ray's scheme. Danette was too forthright and she had too many stars in her eyes when she talked about Ray.

Which meant she was probably hurting as much as Tara was right now…if she'd seen the article.

It wasn't fair. The rat. The absolute rat! She'd like to see him right now and she'd cut off his tail.

"Miss, it's your turn!"

She looked up, realizing from the expression on the faces around her that was not the first time the checker had told her to move forward. Apparently the big chili controversy had been settled.

She tossed the weekly down in front of the checker. "I'll take this, too."

He nodded, his expression bored and then finished ringing her up. She paid and left, anger and hurt sizzling through her in alternating waves.

Those waves took on monumental proportions when she got to work the next day to discover she was being fired. She was told the order came from Angelo's office in New York, but she refused to believe it. First of all, the man was too smart to fire a woman he'd slept with over getting caught out by the media.

Such an action put both him and his company too much at risk for retaliation and a sexual harassment lawsuit, if the woman in question was in the least bit dishonest.

The human resources manager assigned to the task of letting her go had finally admitted that Angelo was currently in Puerto Rico dealing with a natural disaster emergency that had affected one of his supply plants. Apparently even phone communication was iffy.

Which explained why he hadn't called all week.

When he didn't arrive that afternoon, or call, she tried his office. His secretary confirmed that he was calling in only sporadically for messages. Tara left one, bothered by his absence and her inability to get ahold of him. And she had to admit that an emergency like the one he faced in Puerto Rico wasn't something he could dismiss or delegate.

She'd made a decision not to be hampered by her past in every judgment she made. That meant continuing to believe in the tycoon she missed more than she wanted to.

At least until he proved himself unworthy of her trust.

Wanting to get one issue of trustworthiness resolved, she tried to call Danette, but got her friend's home voice mail instead and was forced to leave a message.

The phone rang the next morning and woke her out of a fitful sleep. She'd spent too many dark hours thinking about her best friend and the man who wanted to marry her.

Hoping it was Danette, she grabbed it. "Hello?"

"Tara?"

The voice was familiar, but she couldn't quite place it.

"Yes?" Her voice came out scratchy and she cleared her throat.

"I need to see you, darling."

"Who is this?" she demanded, her sleep fuddled mind sure of one thing.

The voice at the other end of the line was not one of the two men in her life with a right to call her by endearments: Angelo and her stepfather, Darren.

"Don't tell me you've forgotten the sound of my voice. I haven't forgotten anything about you, Tara. I never could. Not the sweet way you smell, or the taste of your lips—"

"I am not in any mood for obscene phone calls," she inserted with speed, recognition finally enlightening her rapidly wakening mind.

Daron's laugh was seductive and low, like he thought she was flirting with him. "How about a visit? Would you prefer I say these things in person?"

"No! Are you in Portland?" she asked, worried that might be the case and wondering how he'd gotten her number.

"Not yet, but I can be. We need to talk."

"We finished talking two years ago."

"Tara, I'm divorcing my wife."

"How fortunate for her," she quipped, unable to help herself. Did he really think she cared?

"I understand your bitterness, darling. I made a terrible mistake two years ago. I want to make it right."

"You don't know the meaning of making things right. You did me one favor two years ago, Baron. You walked away. I'm not about to let you undo possibly the only good deed of your life. You're a user. You suck other people dry and smile while you're doing it."

She had no idea how she'd ever loved this man, but after one week in Angelo's company, the difference between the two types of tycoons was crystal clear to her.

"I don't want you in my life. I don't want you calling me and I swear that if you show up in Portland stalking me, I'll go to the authorities for a restraining order."

"Tara, you're angry, but you don't understand—"

"You're wrong," she interrupted again, not wanting to hear a single line of his con story. He'd deceived her before with that tone and his too believable excuses, but never again.

"I'm not angry. I'm disgusted you could think for one second I would want to hear from you again after the way you used me and then threw me to the wolves in the press with a steak tied around my ankle."

"I can explain that."

"No. You cannot." She exhaled a frustrated breath. "Leave me alone, Baron, or this time I'll be the one giving sympathy producing interviews to the press."

He made a harsh sound. "Tara, you can't trust Angelo Gordon."

So, he'd read the tabloid stories? That was one more thing Ray-the-rat had to answer for. "My private life is none of your business."

"I used to be your private life."

What colossal nerve. "That was a long time ago and it is certainly not true any longer. Goodbye, Baron."

She hung up.

The phone rang five minutes later and when the number only came up as *out of area* on her caller ID, she ignored it.

CHAPTER EIGHT

CHECKING her voice mail after her shower, Tara ground her teeth in vexation when she realized the second call had been from Angelo. But his message gave her her first smile in over thirty-six hours.

He was headed back to Portland and would arrive later that evening. He said nothing about the gossip stories, but he did apologize for not calling when he'd been unable to fly out the day before.

She listened to the message three times just to hear his voice and then erased it with a jab of a button, irritated with her lame, sappy behavior.

The phone rang again, this time a local newspaper name showed up on the caller ID and she let it go to voice mail again. The rest of the day, the phone rang off the hook and the two times she made the mistake of answering it, a reporter was on the other end of the line.

She was in the middle of preparing a tray of snacks for Angelo's arrival and muttering to herself about Ray-the-rat and Baron when something struck her.

What made her angriest about Baron's phone call

earlier had nothing to do with the past. No pain from his betrayal lingered to catch at her heart. No longing for what might have been tugged at her thoughts, but she was furious he had implied Angelo was untrustworthy.

And she was feeling downright feral that her attempt to avoid another phone call from Baron had made her miss one from Angelo.

Baron couldn't begin to understand, because he didn't have a protective bone in his body, but she was sure Angelo wouldn't hurt her. Nor would he allow her to be hurt by others. He was going to be enraged when he found out she'd been fired and she had no doubt Ray-the-rat was going to heartily regret making her and Angelo the crux of his career advancement…such as it was.

Another sudden, not so welcome thought scorched through her consciousness.

She trusted him.

She really trusted a tycoon.

That's why she'd given him the benefit of the doubt about her employment termination. That was why she was waiting for him to show up with a heart full of hope instead of a loaded shotgun. Against all odds, something deep inside of her had bonded with him and told her she could believe in him.

That was scarier than having Baron trying to come back into her life. Her ex-lover posed no threat to her emotional health, but Angelo was something else altogether. She wasn't at all sure how much damage to her current happiness letting him go would do, but she had a feeling it wouldn't be negligible.

She did not want to fall in love again. She did not ever want to be that vulnerable.

Before she started hyperventilating, she reminded herself that trust was not love. They weren't mutually exclusive emotions of course, but neither were they absolutely mutually inclusive.

Were they?

How could she have let herself come to this pass? She'd only spent a few days with him. She knew powerful men like him weren't innately trustworthy. She hadn't needed Baron to tell her that, but when he'd said it, she'd been offended. Was still offended.

Her heart insisted that Angelo was different. Unlike with Baron, she didn't have to convince herself…she had to fight belief. Maybe it was the things Angelo had told her about his past. He hadn't condemned his mom, but he was determined to make the man responsible for her pain pay.

That made him protective, even if it was of a memory.

She should never have researched him. All that stuff about what a ruthless but really fair guy he was had turned her head, or her heart. He'd told her he didn't give up, that he made things work and she had no option but to believe him.

And seriously, a man who spent ten years preparing for revenge didn't change his mind on a whim. If he wanted to marry her, he planned to make it stick.

Was she trying to convince herself to accept his proposal? Or facing the inevitable?

She trusted him, she wanted him and in a way she did not understand, but could not deny, she needed him.

The decision she'd been wrestling with all week was really no decision at all. In a way, Baron's call had put it into perspective. Angelo was nothing like the older man and Tara was sure that if she refused his offer, she would regret his leaving much more than she'd ever regretted her failed relationship with Baron.

The buzzer sounded, scattering her thoughts and letting her know she had a visitor. She rushed into the entry hall to press the black button which would unlock the front door. Sure it was Angelo, she opened her door and waited just inside so she could see down the hall.

Within seconds his tall, muscular body came into view. His eyes looked tired and his skin was pale, but he strode toward her, his body vibrating with purpose.

She didn't smile, didn't speak. She just waited.

He reached her and without a word, yanked her into his arms and kissed her with claim staking intensity. She locked her fingers behind his neck and kissed him back.

When they finally came up for air, she was in his arms and he was leaning on the inside of the closed door to her apartment. She wasn't going to waste time wondering how they'd gotten there. He made things happen.

This was just one of those things.

Nuzzling her neck, he squeezed her. "I missed you, *stellina.*"

"I missed you, too, Angelo."

He lifted his head, his gimlet stare enough to make her heart contract in her chest. "Don't ever buzz your apartment open without using the intercom to see who it is again."

She laughed, relieved that was all it was. "All right."

He kissed her again. Hard and fast. "I mean it."

"I know."

He carried her into the living room and sat down on the sofa with her in his lap. His thighs weren't the only hard things under her bottom. Heat flashed through her, sensitizing nerve endings already on edge.

"You really did miss me," she teased.

He didn't smile in response. "I have severely reprimanded my second in command."

"He's the one who ordered I be fired?"

"Yes."

"Then you know about the articles as well."

"I saw something at the newsstand in the airport."

She cringed at the reminder how widespread was her humiliation. "Did you flip?"

"That's one word for it, but my reaction to the initial article was nothing compared to my fury when I was told you'd been fired as a crisis containment measure. If you were a different woman, that kind of crisis containment could have blown up in our collective faces."

She knew he'd been too smart to take such a step.

"My managers will not act so impetuously on my behalf again."

She shivered at the chill in his voice.

"Why did they?"

His brows rose. "What do you mean?"

"It just seems to me that they had to have some reason for believing you would approve their decision."

"Ignorance."

"Well, yes, but…"

"They were ignorant because they've never been in this situation before."

She waited in silence for him to continue explaining and was surprised when he did after only a brief pause.

"They know only that I hate personal publicity of any kind. I've never dated a woman employed by one of my companies and I don't usually make it on the front pages of the weekly tabloids. My last magazine cover was *Newsweek*."

"I read it. That article had a lot more truth to it."

"No doubt. I'm going to kill Ray." From the way Angelo growled the words, she could almost feel badly for the rat.

"So you think it's him, too?"

"Who else could it be?"

"I can't think of anyone, but I'm sure Danette didn't know about it." Fairly sure anyway.

Once again she was operating on the principle of giving her friend the benefit of the doubt. It had worked with Angelo.

Looking unconvinced by her assurance, he asked, "Have you spoken to her?"

"No. She wasn't at her desk when security walked me out and she hasn't returned my call."

"My second in command will be attending the remedial management training course on human resource development."

She felt a twinge of sympathy for the general manager. "That will be quite the come-down."

"Particularly if you teach it."

She laughed. "I no longer work for Primo Tech."

"This is true." He buried his hand in her hair and brushed his fingers through it to the ends. "That's so damn silky. I'm hoping you'll take a position closer to me."

"What?" First he was talking about her hair and then a job offer? "Are you offering me a position in your main office?"

"In my life."

"You mean you *don't* want me working for you?"

"Of course I want you working for me. Do you think I want a brain like yours going to a competitor?"

She warmed at the compliment, but still wasn't sure what he was driving at. "Um…I'm getting confused here."

"I'm hoping you'll take your next job…working for me…as Tara Gordon rather than Tara Peters."

She swallowed and then plunged. "Yes."

He looked like he'd been turned to stone. "You will marry me?"

"As soon as you like."

"You are serious."

"Very."

"No big production?" he asked, sounding very satisfied.

"No, but I'd like my mom and Darren there, and Danette."

"Done." He kissed her again and this time they were both disheveled and missing some clothes when they came up for air.

She still had her bra on, but her shirt was gone and his was completely unbuttoned. His tie hung over the back of the couch and his suit jacket was in a crumpled pile on the floor.

He was looking at her like a starving man facing a five-course meal. "I want you."

She rested against the hard warmth of his chest. "I want you, too."

"But we're waiting."

"Until we're married?" she asked, an unnamed emotion making her heart squeeze.

"Yes."

It felt right and she smiled, glad that she'd agreed to marry quickly. She liked the idea he wanted to wait, but she didn't think either of their self-control could stand up to a long engagement. "We're going to have one heck of a wedding night."

"Count on it."

The buzzer for the front door sounded again.

"Are you expecting anyone else?"

"No." But she got up.

"This time use the intercom."

She pressed the gray button, thinking she should have done it before. Never mind it being some deranged criminal, what if Angelo had been a reporter? "Who is it?"

"Tara?"

"Yes."

"It's Danette. Can I come up?"

"Of course, hon." She buzzed the entry lock and then dove for her shirt.

"Button up, Angelo. Danette's on her way up."

"Worried if she sees my manly chest she'll swoon?"

"Maybe." She winked. "But mostly I don't want to advertise what we've been doing for the last half hour."

"You're a conservative little soul, all things considered."

She shrugged, but bit her lip. "Does that bother you?"

"No. I was raised by a traditional Sicilian woman, you've got to remember. Before my father died, she defined the term conservative."

"I wish I could have met her."

His eyes clouded over. "Me, too."

There was a knock on the door and Angelo answered it because he was closer.

Danette stared at him as if she was seeing a ghost. "Mr. Gordon?"

"Angelo. I've eaten meat from your barbecue. That puts us on a first name basis."

At that, Danette's eyes filled with tears and her fist flew to her mouth, but the sound of a sob escaped.

Tara rushed across the room and threw her arms around her friend. "It's okay, hon. Truly. We know you didn't have anything to do with it."

She wasn't totally sure about what Angelo believed, but he wasn't acting all cold and accusatory, for which she was grateful.

"But Ray did." And then the sobs escalated.

Tara held Danette until she calmed down and stepped away, wiping her eyes with a handkerchief Angelo handed her.

She took a deep breath and then let it out, her eyes wounded pools in her tear ravaged face. "He doesn't understand why I'm so angry."

"The idiot. I'm sorry."

"Me, too. I broke up with him." Her lip quivered, but she maintained control. "I can't believe I let myself love that slimeball."

"Aw, hon…"

Her gaze darted to Angelo. "I quit my job, too. Told Primo Tech what they could do with their management training program after I found out you'd been fired."

"I'll get you reinstated," Angelo said without hesitation.

Danette shook her head. "Thank you, but I need to get away. I've lived here all my life and been protected for most of it." She bit her lip and swallowed. "I want adventure. I thought Ray was it, but I was wrong."

Tara's heart broke for her friend.

"Maybe I could help find you something." Angelo said.

A glimmer of hope sparked in Danette's eyes. "Seriously? You mean it?"

"Yes."

"Aren't you mad at me?"

"You are not responsible for the malicious behavior of your former boyfriend."

"I'll never make another scrapbook page again."

Tara gave her a hug around her shoulders. "Let's not get hasty. One scheming photographer does not the death of a hobby make."

Danette gave her a weak smile.

They talked her into staying for dinner. When Angelo discovered she spoke both Spanish and Italian, he said it would be a piece of cake to get her a job abroad if she'd like.

Danette left with a smile on her face, despite the sadness in her eyes.

Tara frowned at the closed door Danette had just walked through. "I'd like to punch Ray right in the nose."

"I've done better than that. I've instigated proceedings against him for getting the photo under false pretenses."

"I doubt the charges will stick."

"Maybe not, but I'm doing my best to make sure they do and the experience of going to court and having to hire a lawyer to defend his actions definitely will."

"True."

"So, about this wedding."

"Fly to Reno, get married and check into a swank suite for our wedding night?" she asked, more convinced than ever that waiting would be taxing her control on her feminine impulses.

He grinned, his expression more carefree than she'd ever seen it. "We are going to have a very good marriage, *stellina*. You fit me like a glove."

Angelo looked around the exclusive wedding chapel with satisfaction. A big wedding was out of the question. Not only would it take too long to prepare, but he didn't want the publicity that would accompany it to alert Baron Randall of Angelo's plans to marry Tara.

When he'd seen the innuendo laden articles with pictures of him and Tara kissing, his first thought had been the money he'd paid to bribe Randall's private detective not to mention his involvement with Tara had been wasted.

The whole flight back to Portland, he'd been worried he would only land to discover Randall had gotten to her first.

Randall hadn't gotten to her and Angelo was determined he wouldn't get the chance.

Hence the hasty wedding, but it didn't have to be a shabby, hole-in-the-wall affair. And it wasn't.

He'd offered his second in command a way to get back into his good graces…arrange a wedding fit for a princess in less than twenty-four hours. The wedding chapel was actually outside Reno, in the mountains toward the more affluent and less touristy Lake Tahoe.

The cathedral style chapel was decorated inside with dozen and dozens of white and yellow roses and purple irises. Lit with candlelight and recessed sconces that made the stained glass behind the altar glow, it was the perfect setting for his soon to be wife to walk down the aisle.

Tara's mother and Danette were seated in front on one of the polished wooden pews. Angelo's private investigator and long-time friend, Hawk, sat across the aisle from them.

The music of a pipe organ swelled, filling the space with the strains of the wedding march.

Angelo's gaze snapped to the back of the church where the open double doors framed Tara, her head held high, her dark brown eyes pools of feminine mystery and her hand curled around her stepdad's arm.

They started forward and a wave of something indefinable washed over Angelo.

Possessive desire was certainly part of it. Soon, this woman would be his to have, to hold and to make love to…over and over again.

Tara wasn't wearing a traditional wedding gown, but the designer original filmy white concoction she had on clung to every single one of her curves. It dipped in the front to reveal the top swells of her creamy, smooth breasts. Sexy and feminine, the dress was the stuff masculine fantasies were made of.

Those fantasies vied for his attention with the minister as he went through the wedding service. Angelo managed to give all the right answers, however, and smiled in victory when Tara did the same thing.

Afterward, he took everyone out for a celebratory dinner at the five-star restaurant his assistant had made reservations at. All he really wanted to do was take Tara up to their suite and make her his completely.

The glow on her face made it worth it however. Her mom and Darren were important to her, which was something he needed to remember. It had been a long time since he'd had close family.

After his parents' deaths, he'd pushed away his Sicilian family, only going home to visit infrequently.

"You know, when I gave you that information on Randall, I never would have guessed this is where it would lead you to," Hawk said from beside Angelo.

Tara's mother and her husband were dancing while Danette and Tara had gone to the ladies' room.

Angelo turned, lifting a sardonic brow. "What better way to ensure he doesn't get his hands on her again?"

His friend's eyes narrowed. "I know you can be a cold and ruthless bastard, Angelo, but tell me that's not the only reason you married her."

"Do you think she would be better off having that egomaniac people user back in her life?"

"Tara doesn't strike me as a woman stupid enough to make the same mistakes twice."

"He can be damn convincing."

"Not enough to get her to agree to be his mistress."

"No, Tara would never agree to that kind of arrangement." But once Randall was divorced, the rules would change.

He'd just taken steps to make sure the other man could never again enter the game.

"Do you feel anything for her besides the need to get the better of your enemy?" Hawk asked, sounding like a man with a stronger conscience than Angelo had ever suspected.

"I want her."

"Is that all?"

"None of your damn business."

"I'm your friend, Angelo."

"But you aren't my confessor."

Hawk just stared at him, the look disconcerting, even for Angelo.

"I want her. I respect her. I like her. It's enough."

"I wonder."

"I'm not going to hurt her."

"Have you taken any time to consider how she's going to react once she learns about Randall?"

"With any luck, she'll never have to know about Randall. I'm sure as hell not going to tell her."

"I've never been much of a believer in luck."

Angelo wasn't, either.

CHAPTER NINE

TARA was as nervous as a virgin when Angelo carried her into their honeymoon suite, his midnight gaze burning hotter than any blue flame. The sexual energy emanating off him had been growing all night until she fairly sizzled from the impact.

Despite the elegance of their surroundings, she felt like she was about to be devoured by a mountain lion. A very hungry, powerful lion with sharp teeth and claws that could tear through the barriers she had erected around her emotions.

That shouldn't frighten her.

She'd married him, after all.

But it did.

He stopped on the other side of the threshold, kicked the door shut and then looked down at her, predatory intent and primitive satisfaction exuding from his every pore. "You are mine now, Mrs. Gordon."

"Am I?"

"Yes." Then he kissed her.

It was hot; it was carnal; it was a statement of intent to possess.

His hot mouth molded hers, letting her taste the essence of this man she'd married. Could determination have a flavor? Strength? Desire? Intelligence? Masculine dominance? She could taste all of that and the spiciness of his need in his kiss. They'd never shared a kiss like this and yet her soul responded to it on a level of recognition she could not begin to dismiss.

Swirling sensation spiraled to the core of her and then outward in radiating waves of delight until it was all she could do not to cry out.

He carried her to the bed and stood her on her feet at the end of it and then gave her a once-over that left her trembling. "You are incredibly beautiful, my wife."

"Thank you. You clean up nice in a tux yourself."

His smile slashed through her with heat, leaving her stomach quivering in a way she'd only ever experienced with him.

He reached around her, enveloping her in his warmth and teasing her with his nearness. He started tugging her zipper down. His fingertips played along her spine as each new inch of flesh was revealed.

"Angelo?" Was that hesitant, high-pitched voice hers?

"Yes?"

"Other than the other night, it's been two years and then we didn't…you know."

"Make love?"

"Right."

"You are telling me it has been a long time for you."

"Yes."

"I'm glad."

"Um…that's nice, but I wanted…"

How did she tell her new husband—a man who had married her for the sole purpose of bedding her, or close to it anyway—that she needed him to go slowly? It was so obvious that was not what he wanted to hear at that very moment.

"What did you want, *cara,* this?" He leaned down and kissed her shoulder, nibbling at the sensitive area above her collarbone, before lifting his head. "Or this?" His mouth closed over hers again while his hands slipped down inside her dress and cupped her backside with sensual mastery.

He caressed and squeezed her, his fingers dipping dangerously close to the warm, humid spot between her thighs. Memories surged through her from their time at the beach. Jolts of pleasure zinged through her sweetest spot and her entire woman's flesh. He teased her with his touch, making her want more, making her arch her spine, pushing her bottom back, trying to increase the depth of his penetration between her thighs.

But his hand moved with her, stopping her from achieving the intimate caressing she craved. She moaned against his lips and tried a new tactic, widening her stance so she was open completely to him. He rewarded her with a risqué massage on the highly sensitive flesh of her inner thighs and outer perimeter of her delta.

She groaned at the throbbing pleasure that grew with every tiny caress.

Maybe slow wasn't what she wanted after all. She broke her mouth away, letting her head fall back in abandon. "Angelo, please…touch me."

"I am touching you." His voice was laced with masculine amusement and dark gratification.

He liked driving her crazy. He started kissing her again, but this time, he touched everywhere, but her mouth with his talented lips.

How could she have wanted slow? She was ready to expire and she still had her panties on.

It took him forever to get her dress off, every bit of new flesh revealed had to be kissed, tasted and nibbled until the silky white fabric lay in a puddle around her feet and she stood shivering violently from her need. She wanted to be more active in their lovemaking, but she couldn't make her body cooperate. She was too shaken by the feelings roiling through her with the surging power of an electric blast.

"Angelo, I want you."

"Remember what I told you the other night?"

It was all she could do to remember her own name. She frantically tried to think of what he'd said the night they'd made each other climax.

"You want me to ask?"

"Yes."

With another man, asking would have made her feel like she was begging, but she remembered what else he'd said. "You'll give me whatever I ask for?"

"Yes." The sexual promise in his voice was almost her undoing.

This game made her feel like he was ceding his control to her and when making love with a man like him, that was heady stuff.

"I want you to take your clothes off."

He towered over her, his expression dangerously elemental. "You want to see me naked?"

"Oh, yes."

"Then undress me."

She swayed on her feet. "Is that a dare?"

"A request."

One she couldn't and didn't want to deny.

She started with his tie, undoing the bow and pulling it gently from his neck. She flipped it on the bed, an idea for later forming in her mind.

Then she went to the studs on his shirt, carefully slipping each one from their hole before leaning over to set it on the dresser not far away. The entire time, she pressed into his lower body, swaying side to side every so often to caress the hard ridge against her. By the time she had the whole shirt undone, he was making animal sounds and a white ring of stress had formed around his lips.

"You have formidable self-control.'

"And you are a born seductress."

She laughed, the sound throaty and sensual. "Perhaps…just for you."

She peeled his shirt off, revealing bronzed skin over sculpted muscle that took her breath away.

"Do you work out?"

"Aikido."

"Martial arts?"

"Yes."

"I wouldn't have guessed that of you." He was such

the quintessential businessman, but then it fit with the aura of dangerous male animal that always seemed to be hovering under the surface.

She never wanted to be this man's enemy, but she had no fear of totally infuriating him as his lover—more proof of her innate trust of him on a very basic level.

"We have a lifetime to learn one another's secrets."

"True." Her hand dropped to his trousers. "But even though this is one I've seen once before, I would very much like to explore it again."

"Go for it."

She laughed at the tension vibrating in each of the three short words. "I plan to and this time I want to feel it inside of me."

"Good, because that's exactly what is going to happen." The potent promise in his voice sent warm moisture flooding through the core of her.

He'd ceded control, but not power. How much control would he let her have tonight?

He started to help her with his trousers, but she pushed his hands away. "I want to do it all." She peeked up at him, her breathing coming in ragged gasps that matched his. "Okay?"

"Whatever you like."

"Really?"

"Yes."

She leaned over and took the tie off the bed. "Will you let me tie your hands?"

It was a fantasy she'd had for a long time.

Angelo had gone completely still. "You want to tie me?"

"Um…yes."

"Why?"

"I want to know you trust me."

"And your trust?"

"If I didn't trust you, I would not have agreed to marry you."

"I could say the converse is true."

"You could, but we both know it's not."

"We do?"

"Yes."

He eyed her for so long, she thought he was going to refuse and she was getting ready to drop the black tie. She wouldn't push it. She wanted him and he wanted her and really, she couldn't blame him for being a little leery about her request. It wasn't exactly your average wedding-night foreplay. He didn't understand what motivated her—she needed to know he trusted her. Baron had never trusted her, because he knew how untrustworthy he was. He always had to be in control.

"Do you want my hands in front or in back?"

Her head snapped up at the question, her mouth dropping open in wonder. "You don't mind?"

"I trust you, *stellina*. Do what you like."

He was so darn strong…even acceding to her wishes, she sensed that he was still in control here.

"B—" She had to clear her throat. "Behind you please."

He turned around, his trousers undone and hanging low on his gorgeous hips. Admiration and warmth flowed through her at his acquiescence.

"There aren't a lot of men who would be confident

or trustworthy, therefore trusting enough to let their lover do this," she whispered.

"Not just a lover. You are my wife."

She smiled. "Yes. Your wife."

She pulled his wrists together and tied them, securing it with a bow. It would be very easy for him to undo it, but the illusion of his helplessness was more exciting than anything she'd ever done. Because it was accompanied by a very real faith in her.

She gently turned him back around and finished taking off his clothes. When she was done, she looked her fill at the incredible male perfection before her.

"The other night…"

"Yes?"

"You said if I kissed you there…" She nodded toward his erection. "You would lose control and come inside me."

"Yes."

"Can I kiss you tonight?"

"Yes." This time the word came out more a growl and the hard male flesh in front of her bobbed its agreement.

She dropped to her knees and began her exploration with her fingertips. Velvet encased steel. There was no other description that she could think of for how it felt in her hands. She curled her fingers around him, caressed the full length and he groaned.

"Does that feel good?"

"You know it does."

"For me, too."

"I'm glad."

She nodded and then leaned forward to press a chaste kiss to the very tip. He smelled so good, she nuzzled him, inhaling a fragrance unique to him that affected her every bit as powerfully as his earlier caressing had.

Then she tasted him and he made a noise like a bitten back shout. She wanted to hear him really shout and set about making that happen, using her hands and lips and tongue. His body shuddered and he tilted his pelvis toward her, making his need more than clear.

"You have to stop," he said in a hoarse voice that told her more about how much he'd been holding back than anything else.

She tilted her head back and looked up his beautiful body to his face. Sweat had broken out on his brow and the flush of arousal had darkened his skin.

"Do I?"

"Yes."

"And if I don't want to?"

His arms moved and then the sound of a silk bow tie whispering to the carpet could be heard. "I will have to make you."

She would have grinned, but she was too excited and her mouth was too busy trying to suck in much needed oxygen. He understood her game exactly.

He had trusted her enough to give her control and put him in a pseudo-submissive position, but he was also strong enough to take charge when she needed him to.

"Come up here."

"I can't."

"Why?"

"My legs won't hold me," she admitted, knowing the only reason she was upright was because she was kneeling.

She felt dizzy even in this position.

He reached down and lifted her under her arms, his big hands clasped around her ribs. He lifted her all the way until their mouths were parallel and then he kissed her.

She curled her arms around his head and tried not to faint from a wave of love so profound, she almost drowned under it.

This man was perfect for her in every way. Of course she loved him and it would be okay. He was worthy of her love.

He laid her on the bed and removed the pretty white underthings she'd worn just for him.

When she told him so in a husky voice unrecognizable to her, he smiled.

"You're welcome to wear them again, but tonight, I don't want anything between us, even provocative bits of lace."

She agreed. She wanted nothing between them, either, not even the barrier of unspoken love, but that was one thing she could not remove.

She'd gone that route before, admitting her love and leaving herself vulnerable. She was married to this man. She had all the time she needed to show him it was safe to love her, too, that she wouldn't leave him voluntarily like his mother had done or involuntarily like his father had done.

He made love to her then, starting off gently, but rapidly moving to a passion and urgency that left her sated and exhausted in the middle of the huge king-size bed.

Afterward, he wrapped himself around her and they slept in each other's arms, only to awaken twice more in the night to make love again.

Angelo woke to the smell of coffee and the yeasty aroma of cinnamon rolls. He stretched, feeling more depleted than he ever had from the toughest Aikido session. Remembered pleasure made him groan as he opened his eyes, looking for his new wife.

Tara smiled at him from where she was lifting silver lids from the dishes on a room service cart. "I ordered breakfast."

"It smells delicious."

"I thought after last night that we both could do with sustenance."

"Wore you out, did I?"

"You made me hungry anyway." She winked saucily and he was reminded of her surprising friskiness the night before.

There had been something important to her about tying his hands and he'd worried when he untied them, he would be failing her, but she'd liked that part, too.

A charming, enigmatic, surprising creature was his wife. No wonder Baron had not wanted to let her go. The thought sent a shaft of annoyance through him and he dismissed it.

She'd never be Baron's again. Tara was his now. That was all that mattered.

Angelo clasped his hands and stretched his arms,

then tilted his head from side to side, working the kinks out. "I am hungry, too, *stellina.*"

"Then come have some breakfast," she said breathlessly.

He looked at her and found her beautiful brown gaze riveted to his body. "Ahh…but that isn't what I'm hungry for."

She blushed delightfully and laughed. "That's all that's on offer at the moment. We need fuel. Or maybe you don't," she amended, looking at where the sheet tented from his body, "but I do. Have pity, Angelo, and come eat with me."

He shook his head, laughing in a way he could never remember doing with a former lover, as he got out of the bed.

She was scandalized when he came to the table naked, but almost fell off her chair with laughter when he conceded to her modesty by tossing a napkin down over his lap.

They bantered and made love for the rest of the morning, never leaving their suite until they had to depart for their scheduled take-off time at the airport.

Tara was both obviously thrilled and sweetly nervous when he informed her they were flying to Sicily so she could meet his family.

"Finally."

Tara looked up from her laptop. "Finally what?"

They'd been in Sicily for three weeks, but it hadn't all been honeymoon and sexual intimacy. When she had expressed concern over her career, Angelo had been quick to offer her a dream job and set her up with her own mini office on the opposite side of the study from him in his villa.

She'd never lived or worked in such an opulent setting. What other junior manager worked at a desk that was an original Chippendale and slid her pumps off under said desk to curl her toes against genuine Italian marble? Not to mention having a staff of servants available to care for her every whim?

Was it any wonder she adored Angelo? He spoiled her rotten and every day, her love grew. She was starting to wonder if she really needed to hold back the words until he said them first.

Their relationship was unlike anything she had ever known before and he made it obvious he saw her as an equal, not a woman to be manipulated into being what he wanted.

Her husband's voice had been so filled with satisfaction when he spoke that she wasn't surprised by the look of triumph on his chiseled features.

She smiled at him. "You look like you just bought another company."

"How well you know me." That seemed to give him as much satisfaction as whatever news he'd just gotten. "I haven't, but I'm about to."

Something about the way he said it made her pause.

"What company is it?"

"One I've wanted for a very long time."

"You're taking down the guy who seduced your mom into selling him the family company, aren't you?" She didn't know how she knew, just that she did.

A strange light glittered in his eyes. "Yes."

"How?"

"He's gotten cocky. He never thinks his schemes can fail, but he's wrong."

"In what way?"

"His father-in-law leads a group of investors that make up the bulk of his financial house of cards. Once they withdraw their support, his highly leveraged company will be worse off than a lame duck on the first day of hunting season."

She shivered at the analogy. "Why would his father-in-law remove his support?"

"His daughter has finally wised up to what a bastard the guy is and is filing for divorce."

Just like Baron's little oil heiress…only Baron said he was divorcing her, but she was willing to bet it was the other way around. Unless he'd found a richer prospect. Considering the fact he'd called, trying to see her, she doubted it.

Anyway, Baron wasn't who she needed to be focused on right now.

The strange intensity emanating off of her husband was far more interesting to her. "That makes you happy?"

"Hell, yes. I helped to make sure it happened."

A chill skittered down her spine. "What do you mean?"

"The guy had affairs."

"That kind of man would."

"I took advantage of the fact."

"How?" Then she latched on to his meaning. "You made sure his wife knew about the other women?"

She felt slightly nauseous at the prospect. Angelo's

capacity for ruthlessness was way beyond what she had ever guessed at.

"Yes."

"That was cruel."

"Do you really think so?" His eyes darkened with strong emotions, one of them unmistakably anger. "Wouldn't you have preferred to know what kind of bastard Baron Randall was before getting so involved with him?"

"Sure, but that's different…a wife is already involved. She loved him."

"And he would keep hurting her if she didn't face the truth. They could have had children before she woke up to what kind of man he is."

"You can't justify such cold behavior with that kind of reasoning. You didn't tell her about him for her sake, you did it for yours."

"I didn't tell her anything." He got up and came to lean against her desk. "I made sure she found out through friends, that there was always someone there to comfort her as each new layer of his sleazy behavior was revealed. If my mom had found out the same way, she would have been saved a lot of humiliation and might be alive now."

She wished that were true, but chances were, there had been clues that his mother's lover was an evil man, whoever he was. Just as there had been clues to what kind of man Baron was. Things she'd ignored for the sake of her love.

"I had friends around me when Baron did his public rejection campaign and trust me, it didn't make it any easier to bear."

"You don't know that. You didn't have to face the other."

"No, I didn't, but I did learn that friends can be worse than strangers, or even enemies."

"Do you really think a wife is better off not knowing of her husband's infidelity?"

"No, that's not what I meant at all." But she could see how it sounded like it. "It just bothers me that was part of your revenge against him. I pictured you taking over his company, not laying waste to his personal life."

"No man deserves to be ruined as much as this guy. I'll never forget my mom's sobbing, hysterical confession, or her deep shame and guilt because of what she'd done. His cruelty killed her. You can't get more personal than that."

And it had left Angelo in a world where business and vengeance ruled and love had no place. No wonder he was so ruthless, but he couldn't go on being that way. If he learned to love her, would he soften…at least a little?

"He didn't give her the pills," she pointed out.

"No, just the reason for taking them."

"That could have been as much about her grief over your father than over what this guy did to her. She made the choice, Angelo." She hated saying it, but he couldn't spend the rest of his adult life hating this other man.

A heart full of hate had no room for love and she needed his love.

"Why are you defending him?" he asked sounding both confused and strangely wounded by her words.

"I'm not." She laid her hand on his thigh in comfort. "I'm trying to make you see reason."

"In what way?"

"Revenge can consume you and I don't want you consumed." She pleaded with him with her eyes, hoping he would read the message there and heed it.

He gave her one of the slashing smiles she'd come to adore. "Don't worry, it's almost over and the only thing that consumes me lately is when I get to make love to my beautiful wife next."

"I want that to be true."

"It is. Believe me when I say I spend a lot more time thinking about you than *anything* else."

That was a huge admission and she gave it the response it deserved, standing up to kiss him with all the passionate love beating in her heart.

CHAPTER TEN

"TARA?" They were naked, snuggled against each other on the oversized reading chair in the far corner of the study with their legs entwined and stretched out on its matching ottoman.

Angelo had responded to her kiss with flattering enthusiasm, locking the door and then proceeding to demonstrate just how much he thought about her during the day.

She nuzzled his hair roughened chest. "Mmm-hmm?"

"Why was your breakup with Randall so public?"

The languorous aftermath of their lovemaking dissipated like the steam on a latte. This wasn't something she'd talked about to anyone, even her mom. It had hurt too much.

He rubbed her back soothingly. "I'd really like to know."

"At first, it wasn't. Baron told me he was getting married, but that he wanted to keep our relationship going."

"You said no."

"Right. Up to this point, everything had been pretty low-key between us media wise. The apartment we shared was in the suburbs, we didn't do high profile dating. I thought I was safe from the paparazzi and their blood sniffing."

"Something had to happen to change that."

"It did. I had a couple of friends, or at least they were women I thought were my friends, from the modeling community. They sold the story of my affair with Baron, along with some embellishments, to the press after his marriage was announced. When it became obvious he'd been sleeping with me while courting her, he had to do damage control."

It was Angelo's turn to go stiff, his palpable fury enveloping her. "Painting you as his sexpot mistress who wouldn't listen to the word no, was it?"

"Yes." She sighed, the pain of her friend's betrayal and Baron's willingness to destroy her good name to protect himself only a dull ache, but still there as a reminder to what a naïve fool she'd been. "It hurt so much."

"Because you loved him?"

"Because both he and my so-called friend betrayed me, devastating my life and for what?"

"Money?"

"Right, but it didn't do any of them all that much good. The two models are working fifth string trunk shows and hardly living the high life. Baron's divorcing his wife. Their betrayal didn't take them as far as they expected it to, I bet."

"What?" His hold on her tightened and he went on

before she could answer his question. "How do you know about Randall's divorce?"

"He called me."

"He called you?" Angelo's fury was incandescent now. He sat up, pulling her up so he could see into her face. "Why the hell didn't you say something?"

She frowned at his over the top reaction. "I didn't think it mattered."

"Of course it mattered."

"No. It didn't. Listen, Angelo, Baron might have some idiotic notion about renewing ties, but I wasn't interested."

"You told him no."

"Do you think I would be married to you if I hadn't?"

"What else did he say?"

"He warned me off you as a matter of fact."

Angelo looked a little gray around the edges and she thought that was sweet.

"Don't worry about it. His opinion is the last one I would take on relationships."

"What did you say to him?"

"To leave me alone and then I hung up."

"If he calls again, I want to know about it."

She narrowed her eyes at him. "Don't go all macho controlling on me, Angelo. I'm a grown woman and no one, not even you, is going to boss me around."

"That's not what you said last night."

They'd played a variation on their favorite game the night before with him doing the *directing*. She hadn't minded one bit, particularly when she'd gone to sleep so sated and exhausted she'd had a hard time waking up when their alarm went off that morning.

"It's not the same thing and you know it."

"No, it is not. For that was a game and this is very serious. I don't want you to have anything to do with Baron Randall."

"Do you really think I'm such a masochist I'd want to?"

"So, you believe he could still hurt you?"

This conversation was taking some very bizarre turns.

"No. I don't care about him, therefore he cannot hurt me."

"You said—"

"It was a figure of speech and don't think you're going to sidetrack me from the original topic getting all fixated on it. I'm not your pet dog to order around."

Suddenly she was under him and his lips were hovering just above hers. "Trust me, I see you as anything but a pet dog."

She was relaxing beside their private pool the next day when it occurred to her that Angelo had never once mentioned the name of the man he wanted to take down. She didn't dwell on that for very long because something else came to mind that had the power to blast all other thoughts from her brain.

"Angelo…we need to talk."

The urgency in Tara's voice sent dread skating down Angelo's spine. What could be wrong?

He cut his call short and turned to face her. She was wearing a yellow bikini that set off the sexy lines of her body as well as the tan she'd acquired since arriving in

Sicily. However, her expressive eyes showed none of the latent desire that usually shimmered there.

"What is it, *stellina?*"

"We never talked about kids."

"And this is so urgent because?" Was she pregnant?

The thought sent warmth skirling through him. It had been a very long time since he had been part of an intimate family. He liked the idea of her being pregnant with his child very much.

"We haven't been using any form of birth control."

She was just now noticing this? "I know."

"You know?"

"Well, we were both there." He smiled lazily. "It wasn't something I could miss."

"I didn't notice!" she shrieked, not sharing his humor at all.

"Why are you so upset?"

"What if I'm pregnant?"

"Don't you want to be pregnant?" That prospect had never occurred to him.

There was more of the traditional Sicilian male in him than he thought sometimes.

"That's not the point."

"Then, what is?"

"We didn't even talk about it and for all we know, it's a fait accompli."

"Would that be so bad?"

His question seemed to shock her. "Did you do it on purpose?" she asked accusingly.

He was trying to hold on to his temper, but it was getting harder by the second. *"Did you?"*

"You know I didn't!"

"Look, honey, the last thing I was thinking about on our wedding night was preventing conception. I wanted you so much, you had me tied in knots. Or don't you remember? We were in Sicily before I even thought of it."

"How could you be so irresponsible?"

"Me?"

"*You.* The only other lover I've ever had was Baron and that ended two years ago. Birth control wasn't exactly a blinking blip on my radar."

"And you believe it should have been on mine?"

"Wasn't it?"

"You're my wife."

"So?"

"So, if you get pregnant, it will be a celebration."

"It's not the idea of me getting pregnant that has me worried!"

"That's what you came in here going on about."

"It's the fact you didn't even think about it, which makes me wonder how many other times you haven't thought about it."

"The answer is never."

"But…"

"Contrary to what you apparently think, I'm no more interested in casual sex than you are and since a relationship is pretty difficult to develop when you're working sixty-plus-hour workweeks, I've spent a good part of the last decade celibate."

"But you're not the celibate type."

"A man, even a man like me, only has so much energy. I've poured mine into work." Which no doubt explained his explosive reaction to her.

"You don't make love like a novice."

"Who the hell said I was a novice?" Where did she get her ideas?

"Don't start yelling at me again."

"I wasn't yelling at you." But he had to lower his voice a few notches or he was going to bring one of the servants running.

"If you've been celibate for ten years…"

"I said largely celibate, not…" Suddenly he realized how ridiculous this discussion was becoming. "Never mind. I have never had unprotected sex. All right? You are safe from disease if not pregnancy. By the time I thought of birth control with you, we'd already made love many times. If you do not wish to get pregnant and are not already, we can discuss forms of birth control."

She deflated like a pricked balloon. "I suppose waiting to discuss it until we know if I'm pregnant makes the most sense."

"You're right. Maybe I should get a pregnancy test kit and then we can start making decisions."

"Wouldn't you rather see the doctor and be sure?"

"It takes forever to make an appointment and the test kits are something like ninety-nine percent accurate."

"I'm sure the family doctor will be able to see you tomorrow."

"The big reception thingy is tomorrow night. I'd rather wait until the next day."

"I'll have it taken care of."

"Thank you." She turned to go, but then stopped and spun back to face him. "Angelo?"

"Yes?"

"Do you want children?"

"Very much."

She smiled. "Me, too. I would never consider a pregnancy accidental."

"Nor would I. If you are pregnant, it is a blessing."

She seemed to relax. "Yes. And if I'm not, we'll decide if we want our blessings sooner than later."

"I'm pregnant? You're sure?" she asked the doctor, butterflies taking off in her stomach like Kamikaze pilots on a rampage.

"Sì, signora. It is good we can tell these things so early now, yes?"

"Yes."

She stumbled out of the doctor's office, her mind in a whirl. She was pregnant. With Angelo's baby. Her hand dropped to her tummy. She didn't feel any different, but she carried life inside of her, the product of her marriage to a very special man.

Angelo was going to be thrilled.

In fact, he was ecstatic. *"You are pregnant with my baby? Already?"*

She grinned at his jubilant response. "Yes."

"I guess I am very potent for you." His Sicilian accent suddenly evident.

She pressed herself against him, feeling evidence of

that potency intimately. "Yes, dearest Angelo, I think you are."

He growled and started kissing her.

They flew to New York two weeks later. Angelo insisted she take settling into her new home slowly, sleep late and arrive at the office no earlier than 10:00 a.m. because of her pregnancy. When she argued she was pregnant, not an invalid, he told her he wanted to pamper her.

How could she refuse him?

She was eating her breakfast on their balcony that overlooked Manhattan when the doorbell rang. She got up to answer it, but Maria, the housekeeper got to it before she did.

She halted in the living room when she heard a familiar voice that made her muscles tense. What in the world was Baron doing here?

He walked into the room, his eyes fixed on her in some kind of ludicrous appeal. "Tara."

"You have no business in my home, Baron. You know I don't want to see you."

"I came to save you from a monster much worse than the one you believed me to be." He stood there, looking as handsome as he ever had, but she wasn't moved in the slightest.

She just wanted him gone.

She rolled her eyes at his dramatics. "Godzilla?"

His jaw tautened. "Angelo Gordon."

"My husband is not a monster. Get out of our home. Right now." She called Maria's name. "This man is about to leave. Please see him out."

"Tara, you've got to listen to me. It's for your own good."

She totally ignored him and went back to her breakfast, shutting the terrace door on his voice.

She didn't tell Angelo about the other man's visit when she got to work because she figured later that night, when they were home, would be soon enough.

Looking scrumptious in a dark suit and pristine-white shirt, Angelo came into her office and asked if she wanted to join him for lunch.

She smiled up at him, wondering how much of what she felt for him glowed in her eyes. "I'd love to."

"Great."

They went to one of her favorite seafood restaurants and she was feeding a seemingly insatiable craving for rock shrimp in cocktail sauce when a shadow fell over their table.

"Tara."

She looked up and barely stifled a groan of irritation. "What are you doing here?"

"You need to know the truth about your husband."

"Go away, Baron."

Angelo stood, towering over the older man menacingly. "Leave my wife alone, Randall."

Baron backed up a step, but he didn't leave. "Or you'll do what? Ruin me?" He laughed, the sound hollow. "I'm already ruined and don't think for a second I don't know who is responsible."

"You are responsible. Everything happening to you right now, you brought on yourself."

What was he talking about? Baron was ruined? And

he held Angelo responsible? "What's going on?" she demanded.

"Does she know why you sought her out?" Baron asked, nodding toward Tara.

"Our relationship is none of your business," Angelo bit out, sounding so feral, she shivered.

"Neat evasion tactic." Baron sneered. "But since we both know you detest deceit of any kind, it isn't going to work. Tell her the truth."

"What truth?" But a sick suspicion was growing like a mushroom cloud after a nuclear explosion inside her. "Baron's the man who seduced your mother, isn't he?"

Angelo looked down at her. "Yes. I have more reason to hate the bastard than you do."

Remembering all that he had told her, she could do nothing but agree. "Yes."

But that told her nothing about how she fit into all of it and she was horrifyingly sure she fit somewhere.

Her agreement seemed to take Baron back for a moment, but then his expression turned ugly. "Maybe. But that means she's going to despise you just as much for using her the same way."

Angelo had used her? How?

"You're way off base. Tara didn't have a company I wanted so much I was willing to drive a woman to her death to get it."

The words should have given her comfort, but there was too much tension in them for her to take them at face value.

"I didn't kill your mother," Baron snarled. "She was

weak. She sold you out for a body to warm her lonely bed."

Angelo punched him and Baron went down. "Don't you ever speak of her like that. She was worth a hundred of you and her only weakness was her inability to see you for the selfish blood sucker you are."

Baron got up, grabbing the table for support and then wiped at his now bloody lip. "You think you're so damn good, but what you've done to Tara is no different. You used her to get what you wanted, didn't you?"

Angelo ignored the other man's accusation and put his hand out toward her. "Let's go, Tara."

She shook her head. She'd refused to listen to Baron twice now, but she wasn't walking away from the accusations this time. Her husband had withheld the name of his enemy and now she knew why, but she wanted to know more. Like why Baron was so convinced Angelo was using her.

"What did I have that Angelo wanted?"

"The chance to get revenge on me."

"I already had that," Angelo said deridingly. Then he turned to her again. "It's time to leave. Now."

"But you wanted it all," Baron said before she could react to the chilly command in her husband's voice. "You wanted to take away everything I valued."

"You didn't value me. You dumped me."

"Tara." It was Angelo again. Demanding.

But she was done doing things his way. "Leave if you want, Angelo, but I'm not going until I have some answers. And right at this minute I don't trust you to give them to me."

Baron's look of triumph almost changed her mind. "My marriage was temporary. I planned to come back to you and Angelo knew it."

The man was unhinged and incredibly calculating. He'd married his wife planning to divorce her? Tara shivered in revulsion. "You're not serious."

But she had the awful feeling he was.

Deadly so.

"Oh, yes, very serious. Your precious husband went looking for you the minute his private investigator found out that I was still keeping tabs on you."

The room suddenly felt too warm and dizziness washed over her as the full implication of what was being said hit her.

"*You were keeping tabs on me?* Like some creepy stalker?" She turned to Angelo. "*And you knew about it?*"

Angelo's mouth set in a grim line. "He's had you under surveillance since you broke up. His private investigator had instructions with the incentive of a bonus to squelch any romantic entanglements you might try to get into."

She glared at Baron, ready to finish what Angelo had started. "Who do you think you are, the Godfather?"

"More like a man who doesn't care who he hurts to have what he wants." Angelo's voice dripped acid.

"How did you know about it?"

"Hawk."

"Your friend from the wedding?"

"His private investigator," Baron replied before Angelo could answer. "Tell her how you bribed *my* private investigator to keep quiet about your relationship with Tara."

"I can't believe you've been watching me all this time. That's illegal, you miscreant."

He looked at her like he couldn't comprehend why she was hung up on that detail. She could have told him if he asked. The truth that was being revealed about her husband's pursuit of her hurt so much, she simply could not deal with it. She felt like a million little knives were shredding every happy emotion inside her.

"Tara, Angelo only went after you to get back at me."

Angelo cursed, a word she'd never heard him use, forcing her to acknowledge his presence and the pain slashing at her insides.

She turned from Baron, dismissing him from her mind as if he no longer existed and faced her husband. "The first time we met…you used my report as an excuse to see me, didn't you? You already knew who I was and what I had been to Baron."

Angelo's jaw set with rock like tension. "Yes."

"I told you."

The sound of Baron's voice was like nails scoring a chalkboard on her nerves. She rose from her chair, her body vibrating with unbearable tension and fury, and faced her ex-lover and her husband.

"Listen to me closely, Baron, because this is the one and only time I'm going to say this."

The look of smug satisfaction he'd been wearing disappeared at the tone of her voice.

"According to both you and my husband, he was aware of your bizarre efforts to keep track of me. That means that either he or Hawk has sufficient evidence to support charges being brought against you for stalking. Is that true, Angelo?" She asked the question without taking her baleful stare from Baron.

"Yes, *stellina*. True."

She flinched at the endearment, but kept her gaze firmly fixed on Baron.

He had blanched, apparently finally coming to terms with the fact he had boxed himself into a dangerous corner where she was concerned.

"I want you to leave. I don't ever want to hear from or see you again. If you ever attempt to contact me in any way or resume your pathetic little game, I will not only file both civil and criminal charges against you, but I will make darn sure your wife's divorce attorney has all the evidence she needs to paint you in a light so deranged and amoral, you'll be lucky to walk away from that marriage wearing socks under your shoes. Do I make myself clear?"

"Tara—"

"Do, I, Baron?"

"You've changed."

"And you haven't, but that's not the issue, is it?"

"No, it is not," Angelo answered, his voice colder than an Arctic wind. "The issue is that if Randall comes near you again, the picture you have painted for him will seem like the Elysian Fields compared to what I will do to him."

"I'm leaving," Baron gritted out, "but ask yourself if you should stay with a man capable of using you the way Angelo Gordon has."

The parting words sent wounding shards into her already bleeding heart. She refused to give Baron the satisfaction of seeing her hurt, but what made it hard for her to even breathe was that no matter what sick motivation had prompted his revelations, he had been speaking the truth.

Angelo had used her to exact revenge against his enemy.

She didn't mean anything to him. Not really. And that truth tore through her with all the emotionally destroying force of a level ten earthquake. She gripped the table rim in an effort to stay upright.

"Angelo?" she croaked.

He was by her side in a second, his big hands gripping her waist and shoulder. "Yes, *stellina?*"

"I want to go home now."

She felt like she was being ripped apart. She knew Angelo didn't love her, but to be nothing more than an instrument of revenge for the man who owned her heart was more than she could bear.

CHAPTER ELEVEN

WHEN THEY REACHED the apartment, she went to the bedroom and started packing. She didn't pay attention to what she grabbed, she just pulled clothes from drawers and dumped them in the big suitcase she'd tossed on the bed.

"You are not leaving me."

She didn't acknowledge him with so much as a glance.

Long tanned fingers wrested the top she had just grabbed from her fingers. "No. We are going to talk."

"We have nothing to talk about." Remembering saying those same words to Baron made her flinch. "I'm not staying."

"So, you let him win."

She spun to face him at that, fury so intense she was shaking with it, filling her to the brim. "No one wins in the sick scenario. Not you. Not him. And certainly not me. You used me, Angelo. You lied to me and you promised me you never would."

"I did not lie to you."

"A lie by omission is still a lie."

"No. It is not. Not unless you ask for the answer and I deny it. You did not ask. Nothing I have said to you has been untrue. Nothing."

"Justify it however you like. It won't change what you did to me. Baron is right. You are no better than he is."

"Like hell. I did nothing to hurt you. I am not rejecting you. I married you!"

"To keep me away from him."

His silence condemned him.

"Trying not to lie to me again?" she asked sneeringly.

"It does not matter."

"You're wrong and you're wrong about me leaving. I'm going and you cannot stop me."

"Damn it, Tara, you are pregnant with my child. You cannot just walk away from me."

"I wouldn't condemn my worst enemy to a father with your moral poverty."

It was his turn to flinch. "You would…" He didn't finish his sentence, but she didn't care.

She just wanted out of there. She realized she didn't need her clothes. She didn't need anything but to be somewhere away from him.

She spun on her heel and marched from the room.

He grabbed her shoulder. "Where are you going?"

"Let go of me."

"No."

She yanked her shoulder from his grasp and fell against the wall from the momentum.

His face leached of all color. "*Stellina,* are you all right?"

"What do you care?"

"I care." He leaned back against the wall as if his legs wouldn't quite hold him up. "You don't have to go. I'll leave…stay at a hotel. You're safer here. Please, Tara, let me do at least this much for you."

"No." She couldn't stay where the memories of her doomed happiness with him would haunt her.

He didn't say another word as she walked out of the apartment. She took a taxi to a hotel, checked in and went up to her room to cry her heart out.

She stayed in the hotel for three days, eating room service for the baby's sake, ignoring Angelo's calls on her cell phone and crying until her throat was so raw, she could barely speak to order food over the phone.

On the third day, there was a knock at her door. Her stupid heart leaped, thinking it might be Angelo, but then she told herself it wouldn't matter if it was. She would just send him away. Her heart returned to being a cold lump in her chest.

She looked through the peephole and recognized Hawk, her husband's friend from the wedding. His private investigator.

"Go away," she yelled through the door…more like croaked.

"I can't do that, Mrs. Gordon."

She didn't have the voice to argue. That's the only reason she opened the door, she told herself.

"What do you want?"

"Are you okay? You sound like you're sick."

She shrugged. She was. Sick at heart.

He was carrying a suitcase. It looked like the one

she'd been packing when she left Angelo. Because she had no clothes to change into, she'd taken to wearing the terry robe provided by the hotel with her suite. She was wearing it now, her hair hanging down around her face in stringy tangles.

He put the suitcase down. "Angelo looks worse than you."

Her eyes widened at that. Her husband never looked less than perfectly groomed.

"He's worried about you."

She glared, not buying it.

Hawk shook his head, his expression vexed. "You're both a couple of idiots."

"I am not…" Her voice refused to function any more.

Hawk shook his head. "Why don't you let me do the talking?"

Did she have a choice? She shrugged again.

"I know why Angelo came after you initially. Hell, I helped him do it, but he cares about you now. He needs you."

She shook her head vehemently.

The big man facing her frowned fiercely. "You walked out and I have been with him in that mausoleum of an apartment for three days."

"Not…mausoleum…"

"It is now, with him mourning your loss like a grief-stricken widower. I haven't seen him like this since his mother died. It's always a woman," the tall man said with disgust and shook his head. "Do you know he has not gone to work since you left him?"

When she didn't reply, Hawk sighed with frustration.

"Whether he's too stubborn to admit it, or you are too angry to accept it, he needs you. The real question is whether or not you care enough about him to give him the chance to prove it to you?"

"I'm not too stubborn." The voice came from the doorway and she turned to look, gasping at what she saw.

Hawk hadn't been lying. Angelo looked like he hadn't eaten in a week, not a mere three days. His cheeks were hollow and lined with strain. His jaw line was shadowed with three days of stubble…it was almost a beard and his jeans and sweater looked slept in. But it was his eyes that were the worst.

They reflected the tortures of the damned in their indigo depths. "I do need you, Tara. More than I can ever say with simple words."

"I thought you weren't coming," Hawk said, as if Angelo hadn't just made an impossible declaration.

"I couldn't stay away. I had to see her." Angelo's gaze was glued to her face.

"Well, it looks like she's not faring any better than you."

"My fault." Angelo turned away, his proud shoulders slumped. "I should go."

Hawk said something ugly under his breath. "Don't be an idiot, Angelo. Does she look like she'll be better off if you go?"

Angelo turned back. "I had Hawk bring your clothes. If you need anything else…" His voice trailed off, his throat working like he was trying to hold in some intolerable emotion.

"You," she croaked, unable to let him walk away.

He'd used her and that hurt. So much. But she'd spent three days grieving that pain and there was more here than a man who had callously used a woman to exact revenge. This man was hurting and vulnerable in a way a man like Baron never could be.

"Me?" Angelo asked.

"Stay."

"Very good." That was all Hawk said before walking toward the door. When he got there, he looked back at Angelo. "Don't screw this up. I'm not baby-sitting you through another day of mourning. Men in love give me a stomachache."

Men in love?

Angelo heard the door click shut, but his attention was fully on his wife. She looked like hell and it was all his fault. He'd hurt the woman he loved and hadn't even known he loved her until he did it.

How could it have taken Baron's revelations and their painful impact on Tara for him to realize he loved her?

If he lost her over his own stupidity, his heart would turn to stone. For the last three days, he'd thought it had. He'd hoped she would call, but when she didn't…when she ignored his calls to her cell phone, he'd known what he'd done had been too heinous for her to forgive.

He didn't know why he'd come, except that like he'd told Hawk, he couldn't stay away.

He needed her.

And she did not know it.

She thought he had married her as an act of revenge

and he would give anything to be able to deny that claim, but since he had hidden his own feelings from himself with the excuse, it now stood between them like an uncrossable chasm.

Only he had to cross it. Somehow.

He had to reach her and convince her of his love because the alternative was unthinkable.

He'd lived three days in hell and he knew he couldn't stand one more.

Tara stumbled to a chair and sank into it as she considered the possibility Hawk had been right. That her husband was actually in love with her.

He *looked* like a man who had loved and lost.

He came forward as if drawn by an invisible string and knelt beside her, but did not touch her. "I'm sorry."

"You used me, just like he did." It hurt to talk, her throat was so dry.

She'd left a glass of juice on the small table beside the chair earlier. She lifted it now and drank it down, desperate for the ability to talk this out with her husband.

"Not like him."

She glared at Angelo, not willing to accept anything less than total honesty. "Yes, like him."

"He doesn't feel. I do."

She shook her head. "You can't. You married me to keep me away from him."

"I thought so, yes." His voice was low, full of anguish. "I wanted him to lose everything he valued."

"It worked."

"But I lost more. You never would have gone back to him. I know that now. You are too strong…too smart. Because my motives were wrong, you left me and I don't know how to get you back."

"You want me back?"

"Yes." She'd never heard a single word spoken with so much fervency, filled with such desperation and yearning.

"Because of the baby?"

"Because I love you." Even now, she could tell the words were hard for him to say.

"You don't love me," she whispered in denial, unable to accept that after all the pain and betrayal, he could actually feel what she so desperately wanted him to feel.

"I do. I love you more than my own life, Tara, and I would take back everything I have done that has caused you pain if I could."

"You expect me to believe that?"

"I have never lied to you."

"You would undo our marriage if you could?"

"If it would take the expression of pain from your beautiful brown eyes, yes."

He really meant it…he would give her up if he could undo the past and save her pain.

"The baby, would you undo that?" she pressed.

If he had looked like the damned being tortured before, he looked worse now. "I thought you might…"

"What?"

"Then I realized you never could. Not you and I was glad and I'm ashamed that I was so relieved not just for the sake of our baby, but for my own sake. As your baby's father, I would always have a role in your life. And yet, if I could save you this pain, yes…I would make it so we never met, so you never married me and let me into your body."

If he meant those words then he had to really love her. "How can I believe you?"

His face twisted in sorrow and he averted his gaze, strain coming off of him in tangible waves. They remained like that, her on the couch, him kneeling before her, for several silent minutes and then he turned to face her.

"I loved you when I married you even though I did not admit it to you or to myself."

"I wish that were true." It would make the pain so much more bearable.

"Do you remember our prenuptial contract?"

"We don't have one."

"Wouldn't we, if I only married you to spite Randall? I'm a very rich man. If I didn't love you, if I had the least intention of ever letting you go, wouldn't I have done something to protect my empire? I'm not a stupid man…in the normal course of things anyway."

"You said you wanted the marriage to last. You weren't planning on divorce."

"No, but only love would make me trust you enough to leave something so vital to a man in my position undone."

She bit her lip remembering the prenuptial contract her mom and Darren had signed. The man had been top over tails in love, but businessman first last and always, he'd had one drawn up. It had protected her mom, too, in a way, but still the implication had been the marriage had a chance of ending.

Considering the number of relationships her mom had had between her dad and Darren, his subtle concern had been justified, but Angelo had shown no such concern. And he had a lot more to protect than Darren had.

"You married me to keep me away from Baron."

"I married you to keep you near myself." The urgency in his voice rang true.

"But—"

"Tara, I met you and I wanted you. I got to know you and I knew having your body would not be enough. I've spent ten years spurning emotion, staying apart from my family, never letting anyone as close to me as I allowed you within a week of meeting."

It had been the same for her. "But the revenge…"

"What revenge? Did I do a single thing to Baron Randall that he did not bring on himself?"

Tara considered her husband's words and his need for revenge and realized that he was right. He might have brought the pieces together, but Baron had put them all on the game board. "No."

"If I had met you under any other circumstance, I would have wanted you for mine for all time."

"How can I be sure?"

But even as she asked the question memories bombarded her. Angelo was capable of utter ruthlessness, but he had not seduced her when it was obvious he could. In fact, the whole time he had known her, he had done nothing to hurt her.

He had given and given and given and that kind of behavior from an alpha guy like him denoted she had a very special place in his life.

A place that could not begin to be defined by his need for revenge.

"It is a matter of trust, *stellina*. If you love me, then you can trust me…your heart will beat with mine and know the truth despite what logic might say." The vulnerable expression in his indigo eyes said more eloquently than any words how unsure he was of her feelings, how much she could hurt him right now if she rejected him.

His mom had done that. She hadn't loved him enough to stay and face her own demons, but Tara was stronger than that. If they had a chance at happiness, she couldn't bear to let him go.

"I do love you, Angelo. So much."

His throat convulsed. "Enough to stay with me even though I am not the perfect man you deserve?"

"None of us is perfect, my darling, but I couldn't leave you without ripping my own heart out."

The kiss was a mutual melding of their mouths and their lovemaking afterward was beautiful and tender enough to make even a stone heart cry. Her heart was not made of stone, so tears seeped from her eyelids and Angelo rubbed a wet cheek against her own.

"I have been alone so long."

She held him to her as he loved her with tender, pleasure filled strokes. "You aren't anymore."

"No, I am not." The joy and satisfaction in his voice was unmistakable.

As the pleasure spiraled out of control she cried out, "Angelo, I love you."

His hands cupped her face and he met her eyes, his burning with emotion she'd never thought to see there. "And I love you, Tara. My wife. *My life*."

Their son was born on a spring morning. As the doctor laid the superbly healthy infant onto her chest, Angelo placed one hand on her head and the other on their baby's back.

"Thank you." He mouthed the words, his voice so low it could not be heard.

She smiled at him, this man who loved her so completely. "We are a family."

"Not alone."

"Never alone."

"I love you, Tara."

"I love you, Angelo."

And their baby made a snuffling sound as if agreeing to the preciousness of the circle of their family.

They belonged together, the three of them and God willing, one day there would be more children. Her tycoon would never again have to live in a world void of love and tenderness.

Men like Baron Randall would never understand that gift, but Angelo did.

Because her ruthless tycoon had something the other man did not. A heart.

They're tall, dark…and ready to marry!

If you love reading about our sensual Italian men, don't delay.
Look out for the next story in this great miniseries!

PUBLIC WIFE, PRIVATE MISTRESS
by Sarah Morgan

Only Anastacia, Rico Crisanti's estranged wife,
can help his sister. In public she'll be a perfect
wife and in private, a slave to his passion.
But will her role as Rico's wife last?

On sale April 2006.

HARLEQUIN®
Presents

The world's bestselling romance series...
The series that brings you your favorite authors,
month after month:

Helen Bianchin...Emma Darcy
Lynne Graham...Penny Jordan
Miranda Lee...Sandra Marton
Anne Mather...Carole Mortimer
Susan Napier...Michelle Reid

and many more uniquely talented authors!

Wealthy, powerful, gorgeous men...
Women who have feelings just like your own...
The stories you love, set in exotic, glamorous locations...

HARLEQUIN®
Presents

Seduction and Passion Guaranteed!

www.eHarlequin.com

HPDIR104